PRAISE FOR JAMES PATTERSON'S ALEX CROSS THRILLERS

MERRY CHRISTMAS, ALEX CROSS

"MERRY CHRISTMAS, ALEX CROSS may have a holiday backdrop, but it is a thriller novel for all seasons...One of Patterson's best books to date."　　　—BookReporter.com

"Fans will be enthralled."　　　　　　　—BookLoons.com

"Jammed-packed with action...We see Alex being pulled in all directions."　　　　—AlwayswithaBook.blogspot.com

"His brutal description is spot on and I can honestly say he really moved me in one scene...A great addition to the series."　　　　　—RitualoftheStones.blogspot.com

HOPE TO DIE

"*Hope to Die* is full of surprising revelations, twists and turns, as well as heart-stopping suspense and sharp-edged violence. There is something for nearly everyone here."

—BookReporter.com

CROSS MY HEART

"Twenty years ago, I wrote, '*Along Came a Spider* is the best thriller I've come across in many a year. It deserves to be this season's #1 bestseller and should instantly make James Patterson a household name.' A household name, indeed. Congratulations, Jim, on twenty years of Alex Cross and on *Cross My Heart*, which I am loving. You the man."

—Nelson DeMille

"Twenty years after the first Alex Cross story, he has become one of the greatest fictional detectives of all time, a character for the ages. *Cross My Heart* has got to be the most terrifying and shocking Cross thriller to date, full of unexpected twists, savage turns, and electrifying suspense. This is the page-turner to end all page-turners."

—Douglas Preston & Lincoln Child

"Patterson has never shied away from making dramatic changes in Cross's life, and for this twentieth anniversary book, he pulls out all the stops even more so than usual."

—BookReporter.com

"*Cross My Heart* is one of the best books of the series because it is nail-biting suspense with a surprise twist of an ending... Will leave readers wanting more."

—WestOrlandoNews.com

ALEX CROSS, RUN

"The man is a master of the thriller. He knows how to sell, write suspense, and plot his tales with precision...*Alex Cross, Run* is Patterson at the top of his game...A hell of a read by a master storyteller."   —Breitbart.com

"A shocker...Patterson shows no sign of slowing down and gives every indication that he has nowhere near exhausted his supply of ideas or, more important, unforgettable characters."

—BookReporter.com

"Entertaining and easy to read."

—ReadersRefuge.blogspot.com

KILL ALEX CROSS

"A thriller with family at its heart...It's Patterson at the top of his game."   —Lisa Scottoline, *Washington Post*

"A roller coaster...Classic Patterson."   —*Washington Times*

"Non-stop action...Exciting...The ending is a typically great, surprising Patterson ending that you'll want to read more than once to make sure you really got it."
          —AlwayswithaBook.blogspot.com

"Patterson's narrative style propels readers through the book like a locomotive through tissue paper...Patterson shows no signs of slowing down on any front."   —BookReporter.com

CROSS FIRE

"Fast-paced...The twists and turns will keep you guessing what will happen next and you'll never believe how it all ends... Another great and addicting tale of murder and mayhem— Alex Cross style! I was hard-pressed to put it down!"
          —BibliophilicBookBlog.com

"You don't want to miss this life-changing book...Will leave you turning page after page with endless suspense."
          —BeyondtheBookshelf.com

I, ALEX CROSS

"The stakes are higher than ever before...More than a crime thriller, it's an absorbing family drama."
          —NightsandWeekends.com

"A raw, engrossing thriller that will keep you churning pages long into the night."   —FictionAddict.com

ALEX CROSS'S TRIAL

"A little bit of Atticus from *To Kill a Mockingbird* and a lot of James Patterson heading in a new direction."

—TheReviewBroads.com

"A compelling and unforgettable novel...A powerful drama and a gripping thriller—and the story that it tells is an important one."

—NightsandWeekends.com

CROSS COUNTRY

"The most heart-stopping, speed-charged, electrifying Alex Cross thriller yet."

—FantasticFiction.com

"Intense, suspenseful, emotionally charged."

—BestsellersWorld.com

DOUBLE CROSS

"The suspense, chills, and thrills are there, and an ending which I never saw coming. Another great outing from Patterson, and one that I simply loved. Highly recommended."

—NewMysteryReader.com

"Exhilarating and intense...Fans will be thrilled."

—NightsandWeekends.com

"Vintage Patterson...It is fast moving and suspenseful and takes the occasional surprise twist...Life for a Patterson fan doesn't get much better than this."

—1340MagBooks.com

CROSS

"The story whips by with incredible speed."

—*Booklist*

"Another great one from James Patterson. Hold on to your seat!" —ArmchairInterviews.com

"Smart and straightforward, it builds interest and momentum in short, tight chapters that captivate, creating an addictive read." —TheMysterySite.com

MARY, MARY

"The thrills in Patterson's latest lead to a truly unexpected, electrifying climax." —*Booklist*

"*Mary, Mary* flows effortlessly and with mounting suspense to its final, shocking twist; a fascinating psycho will captivate the author's many fans." —*Library Journal*

"Patterson's hypnotic three-or-four-pages-to-a-chapter pace will keep you up reading far into the night...A great plot twist." —*Fort Worth Star-Telegram*

LONDON BRIDGES

"Exciting...A full package of suspense, emotion, and characterization...This thriller works so well...Any thriller writer, wannabe or actual, would do well to study [*London Bridges*]." —*Publishers Weekly*

"As with the best of Patterson's work, it is impossible to stop reading this book once started." —BookReporter.com

THE BIG BAD WOLF

"The biggest, baddest Alex Cross novel in years." —*Library Journal*

CAT & MOUSE

"The prototype thriller for today." —*San Diego Union-Tribune*

"A ride on a roller coaster whose brakes have gone out."
—*Chicago Tribune*

JACK & JILL

"Fortunately, Patterson has brought back homicide detective Alex Cross...He's the kind of multilayered character that makes any plot twist seem believable." —*People*

"Cross is one of the best and most likable characters in the modern thriller genre." —*San Francisco Examiner*

KISS THE GIRLS

"Tough to put down...Ticks like a time bomb, always full of threat and tension." —*Los Angeles Times*

"As good as a thriller can get." —*San Francisco Examiner*

ALONG CAME A SPIDER

"James Patterson does everything but stick our finger in a light socket to give us a buzz." —*New York Times*

"When it comes to constructing a harrowing plot, author James Patterson can turn a screw all right...James Patterson is to suspense what Danielle Steel is to romance."
—*New York Daily News*

MERRY CHRISTMAS, ALEX CROSS

A complete list of books by James Patterson is at the back of this book. For previews of upcoming books and information about the author, visit JamesPatterson.com or find him on Facebook or at your app store.

MERRY CHRISTMAS, ALEX CROSS

JAMES PATTERSON

GRAND CENTRAL
PUBLISHING

New York Boston

Copyright © 2012 by James Patterson

Grand Central Publishing
Hachette Book Group
1290 Avenue of the Americas
New York, NY 10104

www.HachetteBookGroup.com

Printed in the United States of America

RRD-C

Originally published in hardcover by Hachette Book Group.
First trade paperback edition: November 2015

10 9 8 7 6 5 4 3 2 1

Grand Central Publishing is a division of Hachette Book Group, Inc.
The Grand Central Publishing name and logo is a trademark of Hachette Book Group, Inc.

The Hachette Speakers Bureau provides a wide range of authors for speaking events. To find out more, go to www.hachettespeakersbureau.com or call (866) 376-6591.

The publisher is not responsible for websites (or their content) that are not owned by the publisher.

Library of Congress Cataloging-in-Publication Data
Patterson, James
  Merry Christmas, Alex Cross / James Patterson.—1st ed.
    p. cm.
  ISBN 978-0-316-21068-3 (hc) / 978-0-316-22419-2 (large print)
1. Cross, Alex (Fictitious character)—Fiction. 2. African American detectives—Fiction. 3. Washington (D.C.)—Fiction. I. Title.
  PS3566.A822M47 2012
  813'.54—dc23   2011037879

ISBN 978-1-4555-3571-2 (Target edition pbk.)

ISBN 978-1-4555-4494-3 (pbk.)

For Bob and Mary Simses

Prologue
THE DEVIL ON CHRISTMAS EVE

ONE

THE REAR DOOR TO ST. ANTHONY'S CHURCH HAD BEEN LEFT OPEN. *EXACTLY AS I had been promised.* John Sampson and I eased in through the dimly lit sacristy, the room where the priests dressed for services and where they stored the altar wine, the hymnals, and the vestments.

"Sugar, I hope we don't have to shoot some dude in a church," Sampson said in a stage whisper. "Your Nana'd be predicting me for a slot in the fire."

"Especially if you pulled the trigger in church tonight."

"Not funny, Alex."

"Who's laughing, John? If you shot someone in a church on Christmas Eve and I didn't stop you, Nana Mama would be signing *me* up for a slot right next to you in the big burn."

We made our way along a short, narrow hallway that led to the darkened apse and the altar itself. We stayed in the hall, looking out. Except for some flickering votives, some dim overheads, and a hanging candle near the altar table, there was no light in the church.

There couldn't have been more than three or four people in the place. An old woman clicking her rosary beads, a homeless guy napping in the front pew, an older man reading a prayer book and muttering curses. I carefully checked out each of them.

Then a young girl in a fur coat, a coat way too fancy for St. Anthony's, barged out of the confessional box on the near side of the church. She was sobbing into a long striped scarf. The priest came out after her. Father Harris placed his hand on her shoulder and led her to a pew, knelt by her.

The padre was a very nice guy, and a very good priest, the kind of man you did favors for if you could.

I looked around at the sparse wreaths that decorated the church. I'd been attending St. Anthony's since I was ten years old and I couldn't remember the place ever seeming so bare at Christmas. In fact, the church looked depressing.

I waited until I was sure all the worshippers had their heads down, and then I walked quickly along the front of the altar and knelt at the bottom of the stairs that led up to the carved oak pulpit. The Man Mountain stayed on the sacristy side and knelt among the bright red poinsettia plants, the lectern and the chairs used by the priest and altar boys between him and the pews.

A moment later, the girl nodded and left. Father Harris paused, glanced toward our positions, and then went out a side door.

Except for steam ticking in the registers, St. Anthony's fell quiet. Kneeling there with my back to the crucifix high on the rear wall felt odd and somehow wrong. Then again, the entire thing felt strange. I don't think I'd been at an altar in more than thirty-five years. Not since I had been at that very altar making my confirmation, when I was twelve.

That day, the bishop prayed over us as we were being confirmed, saying, "Fill them with Your spirit of fear, O Lord." It's a prayer that I have always found peculiar because as a rule, I see God as a source of courage and direction, not fear. But I'm not a priest, and so, as Sampson likes to say, what do I know?

We held our positions, in any case, and waited, knowing we had only an hour to pull this off. At six, the priests and friars from the priory next door would come to prepare the church for Midnight Mass. At six, this little stakeout would be over and I'd be going home for a well-deserved holiday with my family.

I have been called cynical more than once in my life. In my line of work, it's often tough to be positive or idealistic about much of anything. But as the minutes passed inside St. Anthony's, I smelled the incense and the fir boughs and watched the votive candles flickering near the manger scene, and I remembered coming here on Christmases past. There was a sameness to the place, a calm sense of the unchanging that got to me.

I felt my muscles relax, and my mind slowed to things that were important, like humbleness and gratitude, which Nana Mama always said were the keys to a long, satisfying life. Seeing how my grandmother was in her nineties and going strong, I tried hard to listen closely when she said stuff like that. Kneeling there behind the pulpit, I ignored the terrible things I'd seen in the year almost gone by and thanked my Lord and Savior for all the blessings I'd received. My wife. My grandmother. My children. My friends. My job. My life.

And as I did, I felt less cynical, humbled by my good fortune. My life was very good. Maybe not perfect, but very good. And not many people get to say that in this day and age, especially at this time of year.

Maybe Nana Mama was right. I needed to come to church more—

A whisper punctured the darkness. Sampson among the poinsettias: "Is this what they mean when they say they're using a cop as a plant?"

I just shook my head. Nothing like a bad pun to help pass the time on a church stakeout. I heard a clatter and looked around the pulpit. The older lady had dropped her rosary beads. She reached over, got them back from the pew in front of her. Then I saw someone come out from the confessional booth next to the one where the woman in the fur coat had been.

He was a young guy, and he was a big guy. He slouched slowly up the center aisle, as if deep in prayer, moving toward the main doors.

This had to be our man.

I signaled Sampson, and the two of us moved forward quickly, eased over the rail into the nave, and began walking up the side aisles, one of us on each side. We kept our right hands in our coats, fingers resting on our guns.

The guy in question stepped out of the church proper into the foyer and stopped at the holy water font. He dipped his left hand in and held it there. A left hand in holy water is a big no-no. *Right hand only*. And the font's no place to keep your fingers more than a second.

Then I saw what I had half expected to. With his left hand still in the holy water font, he shook his right arm, and a pry bar slid out of the sleeve of his coat.

Anticipating that he'd look around before attacking the parish donation and Franciscan charities boxes, I stopped with a pillar between us.

The second I heard metal on metal, I snapped my fingers, got up my gun, and moved to meet and greet the man of the year who'd returned to rip off the poor. In church. On Christmas Eve.

TWO

FATHER HARRIS FLIPPED A SWITCH BACK IN THE SACRISTY. EVERY LIGHT IN ST. Anthony's went on. The man of the year bolted, carrying the crowbar like it was the baton in a relay race. He shouldered his way through the front door and bounded down the steps as the first snowflakes of the year began to fall.

Sampson and I were right behind him, and we were almost on top of the perp before he reached the corner. I got to him first and hammered him with my fist between the shoulder blades. He sprawled hard on the sidewalk. Sampson put a knee on his back and cuffed him. It was done in less than a minute.

I rolled him over, looked at my partner, and said, "John, say merry Christmas to our old friend Latrell Lewis."

"It is Lewis! Holy shit!" said Sampson, and then, remembering he was still very close to the church, he added, "Sorry about that."

Latrell Lewis and I had had some unpleasant history together. It'd started five years ago when he was a fifteen-year-old bag messenger for one of the second-tier Columbia Heights gangs. Street name Lit-Lat, the punk was arrogant enough to try going out on his own and then stupid enough to get picked up by Sampson and me the first week he was flying solo. Next time we took him in, Latrell ended up in a lovely spot in the Maryland countryside, Jessup Correctional Institution, for an eighteen-month swing.

"I'd assumed you were a caged man, Lit-Lat," I said to him.

"Maybe you should learn to count—or buy yourself a calendar, Cross."

We pulled Lewis up off the sidewalk. He was jittery, not just from nerves but from cocaine or heroin or whatever drug he was buying with church money. I really didn't care. I'm a psychologist, but I was in no mood to make a diagnosis and give the man some pro bono counseling.

"Come on. It's Christmas Eve. Show a brother a little heart," Lewis said.

"Yeah, we will," I answered. "We'll show you as much heart as you showed the church and the folks who need that money for food and shelter."

Then we hustled him down the sidewalk toward an unmarked squad car. The wind picked up. The temperature was dropping. You could tell a real winter storm was coming on Christmas Eve.

"C'mon, man. Don't put me in no police car." Latrell moaned. "That'd be sad stuff for the holidays, man. I needed that cash to buy my kid a present. I'm poor, man."

I looked up at the white sky. Then I looked down at this punk junkie and said, "You don't have a kid. You wouldn't be poor if you quit your habit. But it is Christmas, and I don't want you to be sad, Latrell."

He looked up at me, hope all over his face. "Yeah?"

"Yeah. I'll tell you what. On the way to the station, we'll all sing Christmas carols, and you get to pick the first one."

"And for your sake, it better be 'Silent Night,'" Sampson said, shoving him in the backseat and slamming the door.

Book One
MERRY CHRISTMAS, ALEX

CHAPTER

1

THEY SAY IT'S GOOD LUCK IF IT SNOWS ON CHRISTMAS EVE. I DIDN'T USUALLY buy into that kind of folk wisdom, but if it turned out to be true, well, this was looking like it'd be one of the best Christmases ever. A nor'easter was churning its way up the Carolinas at the same time as a cold front was diving south out of Ontario, all the makings for a monster storm along the Eastern Seaboard.

Sampson and I brought Lewis in and booked him. Since there were no arraignments scheduled until the day after tomorrow, it looked like the man of the year would be waiting for Santa in a holding cell this Yuletide season.

It was nearly eight by the time we finished up the paperwork and left.

"Merry Christmas, Alex," Sampson said outside.

"You too, John. Feel like stopping by for a holiday beverage tomorrow?"

"I'll check with my scheduler," Sampson said.

I took a cab home. As the taxi moved through DC, I looked out at the decorations glowing everywhere. The pace of the snow hadn't increased much yet, but the size of the flakes had. They were each about the diameter of a quarter, and thick, making the city look the way it does in those snow globes tourists buy at Union Station and the airports.

By the time I reached our house on Fifth Street in Southeast, it was close to eight thirty. The air smelled of pecan pie. Bree and the kids were busy finishing trimming the tree, which was in the alcove by the window at the front of the house. And of course, the official sergeant-of-all-holidays, Nana Mama, was supervising every little task on her to-do list.

"Don't put two green ornaments right next to each other, Damon. Show some style when you decorate a tree," she scolded with all the authority of the vice principal she'd once been.

Bree was hooking a faded crayon drawing of the Three Wise Men up on one of the branches. According to legend, I had made that ornament when I was in kindergarten, and Nana always dragged it out on Christmas.

"Well, look who's come in from the snowstorm," Bree said, and she walked over and gave me a kiss on the lips. "Hello, sweetheart."

Nana decided not to look in my direction. All she said was, "Is there a faint possibility, Alex, that you might spend a few minutes of the holiday season with your family? Or are we asking too much?"

I should have had the wisdom to say nothing to Nana, to just give her a Christmas kiss, but I'll never learn. She pushes my buttons like nobody else on this earth.

"Thanks for the guilt! All wrapped up in a bow for Christmas," I said, dispensing hugs to my daughter, Jannie; my son Damon, who was home on winter break from prep school; and then Ava, the foster child Nana had recently brought under our roof.

"You're getting a dose of sense, fool," Nana Mama snapped.

"Nana, this morning, when I got that jingle from Father Harris, he told me that *you* were the one who suggested he call me to help catch the poor-box thief," I said. *"Which I did."*

"Father Harris said that?" Nana asked.

"He did. He said that he hated to pester me on Christmas Eve, but you told him it would be no bother. Wouldn't take any time at all for your grandson to solve the case of the poor-box pilferer."

"Humph," she said, shaking her head. "Imagine a priest making up something that. Father Harris of all people. Then again, you never know." She reached in a box, turned to Ava. "Here you go, sweet thing. Put this porcelain Baby Jesus on a low branch, so if it falls, it doesn't fall far."

"So you're saying that Father Harris lied to me on Christmas Eve, Nana?"

She scowled, squinted at me. "I'm saying it's a pitiful state of the world when a man can't be with his family on Christmas Eve. Even a high-and-mighty homicide detective such as yourself needs to be home with his loved ones the night before Jesus's birthday."

Everyone was chuckling at Nana giving me such a hard time. I was holding back a smile myself. So was she.

"Kind of sucks Ali's not here," Jannie said, speaking of my six-year-old son.

"It does," I replied. "But his mom celebrates Christmas too."

Bree said, "I'll be right back," and left the room. I had to admit that the tree looked pretty great against the snowy picture window. Then Bree reappeared with a big glass bowl of homemade eggnog, another Christmas Eve tradition in our house.

The eggnog had big globs of nutmeg-sprinkled real whipped cream in it, so rich and sweet, each cupful would probably register a couple thousand calories. She set the bowl beside a plate of shortbread cookies that also probably registered a couple thousand calories each. But, hey, it was the Christmas season. I helped myself to two rounds of both. Damon got a Christmas-music station up on Pandora, whatever that was, and old Nat King Cole was crooning that all our troubles would soon be out of sight. Even though Nana wouldn't let up about me working on Christmas Eve, it was looking like it'd be a warm, wonderful night.

When the song switched to Mariah Carey's "All I Want for Christmas Is You," Jannie and Ava and Bree started dancing. Damon began telling me about an incredible true story he was reading at school, about Teddy Roosevelt going up the Amazon River with his son.

Then my cell phone rang.

Not even Mariah's transcendent voice could stop that sound from sucking the joy right out of the room.

I hung my head, avoided eye contact, went into the hall, and answered. It was deputy chief of police Allen Chivers. "Am I interrupting Christmas Eve?"

"Yup," I said.

"Hate doing this, Alex. But we've got a bad one. The kind of thing that only you seem able to handle."

I listened another full minute, leaning my head against the wall, knowing just how silent the house had gone. "Okay," I said. "I'll get there." I clicked off, went back. Nana rolled her eyes. The kids looked away from me with here-we-go-again expressions on their faces.

Bree shook her head and said, "Well, there it is, then. Merry Christmas, Alex Cross."

2

AS I DROVE THROUGH THE ALMOST-DESERTED DC STREETS, THE SNOW THAT HAD looked so beautiful an hour ago now seemed downright ugly. It was depressing to leave my house and family, and I didn't blame them for being angry and upset with me. Hell, *I* was angry and upset with me. And with my job.

Goddamn it, I thought. There was only one person in the world who should work on Christmas Eve. And he wore a goofy red suit and drank way too much fattening eggnog topped with nutmeg and real whipped cream. Damn it, and damn Santa too.

As I was driving into Georgetown on Pennsylvania Ave., the snow really began to fall. A bus in front of me hit the brakes in a half inch of slush. I skidded and almost rear-ended it. Goddamned DC public-works folks were home with their families. Let the plows wait, right?

My windshield wipers were icing up as I looked for the

address on Thirtieth Street in Northwest, a neighborhood in the city that was completely the opposite of mine. This was the land of milk and honey, and power and money, and the trophy homes to prove it.

Number 1314 was a beautiful limestone town house lit up like the White House Christmas tree. But I quickly saw that most of the lighting effects came from police cars, flashlights, floodlights, and TV-camera lights. I parked, opened the door, looked down at the slush, and cursed.

I had left home so quickly and in such a pissed-off state that I hadn't had the sense to bring along a pair of snow boots. As I slogged toward the crime scene tape, my ankles got cold, and little chunks of ice and wet snow wormed their way into my shoes.

I showed my badge to the patrolman working the barrier, ducked the tape, and started toward the two MPD vans parked on the front lawn of a Georgian brick mansion across the street. A car door on my side of the street opened. A middle-aged man in a green ski parka and a red ski hat got out and walked right up to me. He pulled off his gloves and held out a puffy red hand.

"You're Alex Cross, aren't you?" he said.

I thought I knew most cops in DC, but this one with the sea of freckles and bits of wavy red hair sneaking out from under his ski hat was new to me.

"I am," I said, shaking his hand.

"Detective Tom McGoey. Six whole days with the MPD. Originally from Staten Island."

"Happy holidays, Detective. Welcome to Washington. I

got just a brief summary from Deputy Chief Chivers. You want to tell me all of it?"

"God-awful Christmas gift for you. And me."

I sighed. "Yeah, I already figured that much. Let's hear the gory details."

3

WE GOT IN HIS CAR, AND MCGOEY TURNED THE HEATER ON HIGH AND FLESHED out the story for me. I soon realized that it clearly *was* a god-awful situation, one with the potential to turn into a full-scale tragedy.

The beautiful town house used to belong to Henry Fowler, a top-flight attorney who'd fallen on hard times. Fowler's ex-wife, Diana, now owned the home and lived there with her new husband, Dr. Barry Nicholson, and her three children: eleven-year-old twins, Jeremy and Chloe, and six-year-old son, Trey.

"Henry Fowler's got them all in there," McGoey said. "He's armed to the teeth and said he is fully prepared to die tonight."

"It's a wonderful life," I said.

"And it only gets better," the detective said. "Melissa Brandywine's in there too." He gestured down the street to another, similar townhome. "She's the neighbor, wife of Congressman Michael Brandywine of Colorado."

"The chief told me," I grumbled; then I closed my eyes and rubbed at my temple. "Where's he? Brandywine?"

"At Vail with his two kids, waiting for her to come join them for their ski vacation. She was supposed to fly out this afternoon but made the mistake of bringing Diana a box of homemade cookies before she left."

Funny what a nice small-town gesture can get you in DC.

"He giving you a reason? Fowler?"

"He's only spoken to us once, and that wasn't part of the conversation," McGoey said. "We wouldn't have known anything if Mrs. Brandywine hadn't used the toilet and texted her husband about what was going on inside."

"The congressman was the first to report it?"

"Yeah, really lit a torch under everyone's ass."

Mentally I began to compartmentalize, to push aside all my frustration at having to leave my family on Christmas Eve and focus on the task at hand. "Tell me about Fowler. His divorce. Whatever I should know."

"Headquarters isn't exactly loaded up with personnel tonight, so we're still waiting on most of the background check. But we know the Fowlers divorced two years ago. She filed, found the new hubby within two months, or maybe before, and moved on. Fowler not so much, evidently."

"Any idea what Fowler's got for weapons?"

"Oh yeah," McGoey said, going to his notebook. "He

gave us the breakdown the one time he picked up the phone."

Fowler claimed to have two Glock 19s. The Glock 19 is the standard-issue service weapon of the MPD, which means I carry a 19. The good thing about a 19 is that it holds nineteen rounds. The bad thing about a 19 is that it holds nineteen rounds. Fowler said he also had two twelve-gauge pump shotguns, two AR-15 rifles, and multiple magazines and boxes of ammunition for each weapon.

Two of everything. What was that all about?

I wrote it all in my notebook, jotted down *Long lead time,* and drew an arrow to the list.

"That everything?" I asked.

"Far as we know. Well, except for the peanut butter and jelly sandwiches."

I frowned and said, "Didn't know PB and Js were deadly weapons."

"Only to someone like Fowler's youngest kid," McGoey said. "Peanut allergy. One bite and he'll have about ten minutes to live."

4

AN IN-FAMILY HOSTAGE SITUATION IS, IN MY OPINION, THE HANDS-DOWN, no-argument worst kind of situation any police officer will ever face. I learned this a long time ago, when I was fourteen, to be exact. A freebaser named Willie Gonzalez took his family hostage down the street from where Nana Mama and I were living. After Gonzalez shot his pregnant wife, his two young daughters, and then himself, I saw one of the police officers who'd been negotiating with him. The poor cop was sitting in his car crying and drinking from an open pint of Jack Daniel's.

I've had the misfortune to be part of a dozen or so of these kinds of details in my career, a few times as lead negotiator, more often as a psychological consultant. There's a broad spectrum of things that can happen when you're a cop: You might have to sharpshoot a terrorist. Or meticulously unravel a kidnapping. Or even outfox a serial killer or two. Any of these situations can mess you up psychologically.

But dealing with someone holding family members hostage is like trying to stop a Mack truck carrying a full load of insanity. Usually the person with the gun—more often than not, it's an obsessive, substance-abusing male, like Willie Gonzalez—is so far gone he doesn't give a damn about his hostages, or his future. He blames them for something. He blames himself for something. He can't get his facts straight or see the truth of his circumstances. It's a lose-lose situation all the way around.

As for hostage negotiators, well, we are usually smart and well trained, but we rarely pull off the heroics you see in movies. Have I ever seen the abductor listen to the negotiator and then throw down his weapon and come out with his hands up? Sure, about as often as I've seen the Redskins win the Super Bowl. Two or three times. It's in the realm of possibility. But the odds are stacked against it.

We got out of the car and headed toward the police vans where McGoey said officers were trying to reestablish contact with Fowler. Nearly an inch of snow had fallen and the storm was only getting worse. My feet began to freeze again.

"Think they have an extra pair of boots?"

The detective looked at my shoes and said, "I've only been here six days."

"Good point," I said, thinking that I really did not like cold and snow. "Whose property is this?" I asked, indicating the Georgian brick mansion his car was parked in front of.

"Ambassador from Nigeria. No idea how to pronounce the name."

"Nice place the ambassador from Nigeria's got."

"Yeah, half his country is starving to death, and this dude's living in six bedrooms in Georgetown. Guess he's gone for the holidays too."

"Probably to Lagos. I've been there. A real hellhole. Then again, from the look of things, maybe I'd rather be in Lagos tonight myself."

5

A GOOD FRIEND OF MINE, LIEUTENANT ADAM NU, WAS THE SWAT COMMANDER on duty that night. He was the kind of guy who was always thinking ahead. After hearing the weather report earlier, he'd ordered his men to erect tarps and wind blocks behind the two MPD vans. They'd put down outdoor carpet over the snow already on the ground, then run extension cords and put lights up as well. A gas-fired construction heater had been brought in and was blowing two hundred thousand BTUs as members of his team sorted their gear. And he had an extra pair of black tactical boots and wool socks.

"You certainly know how to prepare for a blizzard, Adam," I said, sitting on a bench inside the makeshift shelter and changing socks.

"Raised in Duluth by a father who loved ice fishing," Nu said, shrugging.

"You have men already deployed?" I asked.

Nu confirmed that he had several men set up at different distances and places around the Nicholsons' house. The snow made it impossible to put our people on the roofs of the adjacent homes, the ideal locations. But he had men trying to track down the absentee owners to get permission to enter their homes. That way, the officers could take up window positions, where they might be able to peer inside the Nicholsons' residence with binoculars or thermal imaging systems.

Nu also had heavily armored SWAT officers constantly circling the house along the perimeter of the property. They each carried a SIG SAUER P226, a high-powered rifle with precision location.

"Shouldn't those guys be set up to snipe?" McGoey asked.

"I have enough," Nu said. "And FBI research has shown that moving men keep the perp off balance. Sometimes confuses him into revealing himself."

"Floor plans?" I asked.

"Ramiro's got a copy inside," Nu said, and we entered the van on the left.

Detective Diego Ramiro, another friend, as well as a hostage negotiator with far more experience than me, was one of three people in the van who were speed-dialing the landline inside the Nicholson home and the cell phones belonging to the doctor, his wife, and the wife of Congressman Brandywine.

For all we knew, Fowler had seized all phones. For all we knew, Fowler enjoyed the nonstop ringing. That's just how variable and bizarre these family hostage situations can be.

Ramiro, a thickly built guy in his early fifties, punched off his own cell, looked at me in extreme frustration, and said, "Alex, we can't do a goddamned thing if this son of a bitch won't pick up his phone and talk to us."

I'd worked with Ramiro before. He wasn't one to lose his cool. Then again, like me, like everyone there, he wasn't home on Christmas Eve. We were all stuck in a blizzard, waiting for a lunatic to answer the phone.

I said, "How long have we been calling Fowler?"

Diego flipped through his notepad. "We started almost an hour ago."

McGoey said, "That's when Fowler was real chatty about who he had in there and what kinds of guns and ammo he had."

"Keep talking to him," I said. "Leave messages. Every single time."

Ramiro nodded, gave the order to the others. I sat there listening for several moments, wishing to God I had more information on Fowler. What had taken him from a life as a wealthy attorney to this desperate hour?

I'd no sooner asked myself that question when Ramiro waved his finger at me and McGoey, then hit a button on his mobile. It was connected wirelessly to speakers inside the van. We heard a woman's muffled voice, noises, and then a whimper. We held our breath and stared at the speakers as if they were video monitors.

"Mr. Fowler?" Ramiro began. "Thank you for—"

Gunshots exploded on the other end of the line.

The Christmas horror show had begun—or maybe it had just ended.

CHAPTER

6

DAMON STOOD ON TIPTOES ON A WOBBLY KITCHEN CHAIR. HE WAS SWEATING AND trying very hard to hook a delicate antique angel to the top of the Christmas tree.

"I'll get a stepladder, get up there myself," Nana Mama said.

"I don't need a stepladder and I'm certainly not letting my ninety-year-old great-grandmother use one," Damon shot back.

"You're just lazy," Nana Mama declared. "Your father raise you like that, or are you majoring in that subject at that fancy prep school you go to?"

Damon didn't know whether to be angry or start laughing at the fact that she was busting his chops like this. At last his fingers secured the angel to the tree with a piece of ancient white lace Nana Mama said had belonged to her grandmother.

"There," he said, jumping off the chair and looking at the old woman. "A little applause?"

"For what?" his great-grandmother asked.

"For getting the angel up there?"

"Oh, that," she said. "You'd have gotten me that stepladder, I'd have done it myself a lot quicker."

"And broken your hip," Bree said as she began packing up the ornaments and lights that had not made the tree this year. "Thank you, Damon. She looks beautiful up there."

Nana Mama sighed, said, "I don't understand why the top of the tree is always the last thing we decorate. It should be the first, so the angel can look down on us while we decorate the tree. That makes perfect sense, doesn't it?"

Damon didn't reply. No one replied. No one except Nana Mama had felt much like talking since Alex left.

But Nana just kept going. "Jannie, what do you think?" she asked.

"With all due respect, Nana," Jannie said, "I think that you think that if you keep talking, we'll forget Dad is out on a case and might get hurt on Christmas."

Nana walked to Jannie and hugged her tightly. "You are one smart girl, Jannie. Smart women run in this family."

Damon rolled his eyes. Bree smiled slightly, and Nana tried her hardest to snap back into her sensible self. She said, "That Alex. He's my fault. I admit it: I didn't raise that boy right. If I had, he'd never be foolish enough to go out on a nasty case on Christmas."

Again, nobody said a word.

Then Bree looked up from her packing and said, "Listen. It's pretty obvious that Alex won't be home for a while. Maybe quite a while. So let's just make the best of it. Merry Christmas to all."

Ava added, "And to all a good night."

Nana tried to smile, but her eyes filled with tears. "Yes," she choked out. "A good night. Please, dear Lord, let it be a good night."

Damon melted, went to his great-grandmother, hugged her, and said, "It will be, Nana. I promise you, it will be."

7

THE SOUNDS OF THE SIX RAPID-FIRE GUNSHOTS RANG IN MY SKULL.

Six hostages, I thought. Was it over? Were we looking for bodies?

And then we heard the hysterical cries of children. "Daddy, no!"

They were quickly drowned out by an angry and ugly voice blaring over the speakers in the van: "I could have taken out every one of these sad excuses for humanity, each and every one of these sad pieces of shit. But I didn't. You know why? Because you don't unwrap your presents on Christmas Eve. You wait until the high holy day of consumerism to do that. Isn't that right? Well, not this time, folks! I just unwrapped them all!"

Fowler started laughing like a happy madman.

"Please, Daddy!" a girl's voice sobbed. Chloe Fowler.

"Please what?" Fowler snarled. "'Please don't shoot

Barbie, Daddy? If you shoot Barbie, who will Ken love, Daddy?'"

A male voice was then heard. Dr. Nicholson. "You're terrifying her, Fowler. She's your own daughter."

"No!" Fowler snorted derisively. "Is that right, *Barry?* You know everything, don't you, *Barry?* Mr. Optometrist—fucking cash-flow doctor of the year."

A gun blasted. We heard glass breaking and more crying.

Fowler was shouting. "See that? See that, Mr. Optometrist? Shut the hell up, Mr. Optometrist! Or you're going to look just like everything else under the Christmas tree." He began to sing: "'O Tannenbaum, O Tannenbaum!'"

"Mr. Fowler!" Ramiro yelled into his phone.

"'How lovely are thy branches!'" Fowler sang, and then he stopped. We heard footsteps. The phone was picked up.

Fowler whispered, "What did old Henry the magic man and his magic wand take out, ladies and gentlemen of the jury? Anyone? Anyone?"

He paused. McGoey, Nu, and Ramiro glanced at me, confused. Before I could even think about how to interpret Fowler's ravings, he said, "Awww, let's see. A nice new iPad. Got it right in the apple...and here we have what used to be an Xbox Kinect. Ladies and gentlemen of the jury, plaintiff should be thanking me, not suing me. Now my idiot sons will have more time for homework. And my ex-wife's Tiffany bauble? I mean, c'mon, have you ever seen such overpriced crap? There ought to be a law against Tiffany and Nordstrom. I mean, look at that beautiful blue polo sweater of Barry's. Cashmere does not stop buckshot, now, does it, ladies and gentlemen?"

Fowler stopped talking. All we could hear was his rushed breath, and I wondered if he was on drugs or drinking or both.

"Hey, Mr. Fowler," Ramiro said calmly, carefully, almost softly—the way they teach you in the FBI courses about hostage negotiation.

"Who the hell are *you?*" Fowler shot back.

"My name is Ramiro. I'm glad to hear that the people you've got in there are okay. That's good news."

Fowler exploded: "What are you, *another whiny-ass cop?* These people in here are *not* doing okay, Officer Whiny Ass. Once the sun rises and all the Cindy Lou Whos down in Whoville have sung their song, I'm going to blow their heads off once and for all."

The children began to cry again.

Ramiro glanced at me. I made a downward motion with my hands. Stay calm. Do everything calmly.

"I understand what you're saying, Mr. Fowler," Ramiro said. "How about we talk, work things out?" *Good,* I thought. Calmly engage him. Establish common ground.

"You some kind of hostage negotiator?" Fowler asked.

Ramiro hesitated. Not a good thing. He said, "I'm just a guy who wants to hear what you have to say, Mr. Fowler."

"Tell it to the jury, whiny ass!" Fowler shouted. "I am never talking to you ever again. *Ever.*"

Click.

8

OUTSIDE, THE WIND BEGAN TO PICK UP, SLASHING THE SNOW SIDEWAYS. THE lawn in front of the Nicholsons' house had disappeared beneath the three inches that had already fallen.

"How do we handle this guy, Alex?" Ramiro said. "He sounds psychotic."

"Or wasted on something stronger than pathological rage," I said.

Adam Nu was on the phone with Congressman Brandywine, assuring him that as far as we knew, his wife was still alive among the hostages inside. I studied the notes I'd jotted down after Fowler hung up, trying to see some kind of pattern to his ravings.

He'd talked to us as if we were the jury and he were arguing his case in civil court. He admitted shooting the Christmas presents. He'd called his ex-wife's husband "Mr. Optometrist—fucking cash-flow doctor of the year." He clearly loathed Barry Nicholson. He clearly had deep-seated money resentment. Called Christmas the "high holy day of consumerism." Ranted about Tiffany. He had even referred to Cindy Lou Who and Whoville, from the Grinch story.

Was that how he saw himself, in some deluded way? As the Grinch? I tapped on the notebook and realized something. I hadn't heard the two women, had I? Maybe one there, right at the outset, before Fowler started shooting. But from that point onward, no women's voices at all. Were they dead?

No. He would have made a reference to shooting them. So they were there, but not talking. Why? So they didn't disturb—

"Alex," McGoey said.

I looked up. The detective handed me a computer tablet, said, "Guys downtown just sent over the file on Henry Fowler."

Nu got off the phone with the congressman. The three of us used separate tablets to scan through the police reports, psychological evaluations, and clippings that Henry Fowler had generated on his way to a hostage standoff. I skipped his rap sheet for the moment, wanting to understand who he had been before all this. In some ways, it was like taking a walk with the Ghost of Christmas Past.

9

FOWLER'S EARLY DAYS OVERFLOWED WITH PROMISE. BORN INTO A MIDDLE-CLASS family of teachers, he'd attended New Trier High, apparently a good public school in the Chicago suburbs, then gone to Georgetown for his undergraduate degree, and Georgetown Law after that. The MPD had even managed to dig up Fowler's college yearbook photo. He had graduated third in his class, and it sure didn't hurt that he looked like he could be Tom Brady's brother.

After law school, Fowler landed at Fulton Holt, one of the best white-shoe law firms in the nation's capital. Fowler quickly became well known. He had the perfect combination of traits for a civil defense lawyer: unrelenting stamina, classical eloquence, and a killer attitude.

There were fawning pieces on him in the *Post* and the *Times*. Reading them, I realized that I had heard of the man. Years ago, nine hundred women had joined a class-action suit against a national retail chain, charging the chain with noncompetitive wages and workplace harassment.

Bree and I had talked about the case on one of our first dates. Hardly romantic, I know, but my yet-to-be wife had followed the case almost obsessively because she'd worked at the company before entering the police academy. She believed the women had been unfairly treated because she herself had been unfairly treated at that job.

Fowler had represented the retail chain in the suit, however. And Fowler had won. But the articles all noted that Fowler's forte was not workplace law; he specialized in wrongful-death pharmaceutical cases.

Prior to the workplace lawsuit, he'd represented a California biotech company being sued by relatives of people who'd participated in a trial of a new Huntington's disease drug and died shortly after treatment. Fowler had argued convincingly that the patients in question had been terminal at the time of the study, that they'd been hoping for miracles, and that his client could not be held liable for not delivering miracles.

Fowler went back to pharmaceutical litigation after the big workplace decision. He was hired to defend a member of Big Pharma against charges that its new hepatitis A vaccine caused neurological damage in 10 percent of patients.

Fowler won again. The drug stayed on the market.

"He must have made a fortune from that," I said.

McGoey nodded. "Paid a million in taxes that year. Do the math."

"He's flush at that point," agreed Nu, who was looking at his own screen. "But then a few years ago, something happens. It all starts to unravel."

10

"WHERE ARE YOU SEEING THAT?" I ASKED NU. "DIVORCE RECORDS?"

"That's sealed," the SWAT lieutenant said. "But have you looked at the rap sheet yet, Alex? This guy doesn't hit the skids slow. He walks right off a cliff."

I went back, found the sheet, opened it, and quickly saw what Nu was talking about. About a year before his wife filed for divorce, Fowler was arrested on a drunk-driving charge. Prior to that, he'd never been in trouble with the law. That changed in a big way over the course of the next six months.

During that time he was charged with two more DUIs and lost his license. That didn't stop him. He was spotted buying drugs in Anacostia at one point; stopped and arrested with meth and black-tar heroin in his possession at another. A month after that, he was arrested on charges of beating a hooker; he'd done it while wasted, blaming her for who he'd become.

At least seven times, Metro police were called to the Fowler residence by neighbors complaining of domestic disturbances. Nine months into his radical new behavior, Fowler lost his job, voted out by his partners. Two months after that, Fowler's wife changed the locks on the house, got a restraining order barring him from contact with her or her children, and filed for divorce.

That action had only driven Fowler further away from his former self. Not a month went by without something interesting to report about the counselor. Charges of attempting to intimidate a witness in his divorce trial. Charges of child abuse by his wife. Illegal possession of firearms.

The night his divorce became final, Fowler broke into a former friend's house and stole whatever he could lay his hands on. He was arrested and spent ninety days in jail, his first real stretch, but not his last.

His ex-wife announced her intention to wed Dr. Barry Nicholson, an old friend of the family, and a week later, Fowler showed up at the optometrist's office high on a handful of substances and carrying a knife. He threatened Nicholson and terrorized the staff at the doctor's office for almost an hour before being arrested and subdued.

Nicholson had refused to press charges, stating that he believed Fowler was mentally ill and that his radical change in behavior was the result of something organic rather than environmental. The court ordered Fowler held for a psychiatric review, but nothing conclusive was found and he was ultimately released.

Next, Fowler tried to disrupt his ex-wife's wedding. Guards caught him and escorted him out, but he could be heard shouting that Barry Nicholson was doomed and that his ex-wife was doomed. Since then, Fowler's life had turned even more squalid and desperate.

To support his habit, Fowler tried to become a drug dealer. He was not successful and lived on the street for a while, the usual elegant lodgings—dumpsters, abandoned houses, public restrooms. Then a third-rate hooker who called herself Patty Paradise took him in. Patty was a pathetic druggie herself, afflicted with the shakes, rotted teeth, HIV, the whole catalog of problems that accompany meth addiction.

Fowler had recently spent four months in jail in Montgomery County, Maryland, on burglary charges.

"He got out the day after Thanksgiving," McGoey observed. "Which gave him a solid twenty-eight days to get ready for this."

"Unless he was preparing before that," I said, rubbing my temple. "As an old boss of mine used to say, 'There's no rest for the wicked and no snooze button on the human time bomb.'"

11

IN THE HOUR THAT FOLLOWED, FOWLER NEVER ONCE PICKED UP THE PHONE. BUT members of Adam Nu's team got hold of snow camouflage and crept close to the house with listening devices. They returned around ten minutes to eleven, and I recommended that Tom McGoey call a quick meeting of the minds.

We gathered outside the two vans in that makeshift shelter, which was surprisingly warm and dry, given the weather around it.

"He's into hour four holding the hostages by himself," I began. "This is not a good thing. With a partner, Fowler can sleep. Without a partner, each minute gets more difficult for him. He's got to monitor the people he's holding. He's got to be suspicious of every creak in the floorboards."

One of the SWAT guys who was wearing the snow

camouflage, a small, tough-looking officer named Jacobson, said, "He's whacked on something."

"You had visual on him?" McGoey asked.

"For a second, when we tried to place a listening device. Fowler moved through our line of sight carrying his works."

"What's he shooting?" I asked.

"He's moving fast, jittery," Jacobson said. "My bet's meth."

It made sense. In jail these days, meth was passed around like hors d'oeuvres at a party. In the past few years it had become just as popular on the streets of DC. And Fowler was a known user.

"Okay, so depending on how long he's been on this particular tweaking binge, he could go rhino on us at any moment," Nu said.

A meth addict on a binge is chaos walking and talking. In the first day or two, his emotion swings. Gregarious one moment. Paranoid the next. Euphoric, and then drowning in the depths of depression. At a certain point, however, usually after he's spent many days awake, the drug triggers a bout of wild rage, and the tweaker goes rhino trying to destroy anyone and anything around him.

"Any sense of how close we are to that?" I asked Jacobson.

The SWAT officer shook his head. "Not from what we saw."

"Do we have the listening device planted?" McGoey asked.

Jacobson shook his head again. "Too much snow and

ice. We were nervous that if he heard us try to clean the outer window, he might open fire on the hostages."

"Smart," I said.

Nu informed us that his men had been able to get permission to enter the homes adjoining the Nicholson residence and were already moving into position.

"I'm putting two snipers to a house, and assault teams in range of every door—front, back, patio, kitchen, garage. If we can distract Fowler at the front door— where these kinds of guys tend to concentrate their attention—we may be able to go in through the back."

"Alarm system?" I asked.

"Good point," Nu said. "I'll have it shut down."

The discussion had turned to going after Fowler. It frustrated me, but if the man wasn't going to talk to us, what else could we do?

"Let's talk about timing," McGoey said. "I think the longer we wait…"

I noticed something that made me stop listening to him in the middle of his sentence. I saw, over Nu's shoulder and out through a slit in the tarps, a bundled-up woman tromping through the four inches of snow that now coated the city. She was walking right toward us. I caught a glimpse of her face in a flashlight beam.

It was Bree.

What was wrong? Why was my wife here?

12

"EXCUSE ME, GENTLEMEN. I'LL BE RIGHT BACK," I SAID AS I BROKE AWAY FROM the group, and Bree entered the shelter.

"Hey," I said, going to her. "What's wrong?"

She drew back her hood.

"*Wrong?*" Bree asked in a whisper. "When I left the house, Nana was crying her eyes out, sure that you were going to die on Christmas Eve."

My stomach churned. "Look, I'm fine. You can see for yourself. I'll call her."

"She's gone to bed."

"Which is where you should also be."

"Do you think I could possibly sleep, Alex?"

I sighed. "Bree, you of all people know how this works."

"I know how it works for you," she said. "I can say no

to the job but you can't, Alex. That's not good for you or your family. Especially at Christmas."

"Sometimes you can't say no, even if it is Christmas," I said. "Sometimes you have a lunatic meth head who decides that the holiday is a perfect time for him to take his ex-wife, their three kids, and her new husband hostage."

Bree hugged herself, looked away, and said, "You have a family who all feel like other families in a crisis come first for you."

"That's not fair, Bree."

"Maybe not," she said, looking back at me. "But I thought it was important that you know that your children think that."

My head felt heavy. So did my chest. I said, "I am sad beyond words to hear that, Bree. And there is nothing I want more at this moment than to go home right now and then get up in the morning tomorrow and unwrap presents. But I honestly don't know how I'd live with myself if I did that and then heard that this guy murdered his entire family when I might have been able to prevent it."

Bree gazed at me; she reached up and touched my cheek with her chilled fingers. "You've got to do what you've got to do. I just want you to remember that there are consequences to everything."

I nodded, wondering if our relationship was starting to suffer the consequences of me being me. "I love you," I said. "And I have to go back to work so I have a chance of being with my family on Christmas morning."

My wife's eyes were filled with a mixture of understanding and resignation. She touched my cheek again. Then she turned away and left the shelter. I went out into the storm and called after her, "Be careful driving."

She called back over her shoulder, "I'll pray for you, Alex. It's all I can do."

13

BREE KEPT WALKING AND DISAPPEARED BEHIND THE POLICE BARRIER INTO THE storm. I stood there, staring after her, my mind whirling with thoughts of my family.

What was I doing? Ramiro and Nu and McGoey were all first-rate at their jobs. The deputy chief had called me in part, I guessed, as a way to calm down the congressman. But did I really have to be present? Couldn't I leave this situation in their capable hands and follow Bree home?

"Alex!" McGoey called.

I turned, squinted into the wind and the snow, and saw him standing at the flaps of the tent.

"It's Fowler," he said. "He picked up. He wants to talk to you."

"Me?" I replied, already moving toward him, already compartmentalizing.

"He didn't ask for you exactly," McGoey said. "Just anyone but Ramiro."

I walked through the shelter, brushing the snow off my hat and jacket, and climbed into the van, trying to fully move on from my conversation with Bree. I had to completely divorce myself from the sadness and anxiety she'd stirred in me. If I didn't, I'd be in no condition to negotiate with a madman.

Ramiro handed me his phone.

"Henry Fowler?" I said.

He coughed. "Who's this?"

"My name is Alex Cross," I said.

There was a long pause before he said, "I've heard of you."

"And I've heard of you," I said. "You're an impressive man, Mr. Fowler."

He laughed acidly at that. "I'm a fucking loser, Cross. Let's call it what it is, because I am, in no way, the man I was."

"If you say so," I replied, then paused. "So what are we doing here?"

"We?" Fowler said. "There's no *we* here. There's just you, Cross, and all your well-armed friends out there, the members of the jury, looking to spoil my fun."

Fun. I shut my eyes. That wasn't what I wanted to hear. It meant that he planned to toy with his hostages and us. He would enjoy that, so he would try to draw out the experience. This was looking like it was going to be a long Christmas Eve night.

"Is that what this is, a game?" I asked. "Or a trial?"

"Both," he said in a reasonable tone. "That's what a trial is, isn't it? A game played with deadly intent?"

"I suppose."

"You suppose. Before we move on, Cross, a word of advice."

"Yes?"

Fowler began screaming: "Don't fuck with me! Don't lie to me! And don't try to game me. If you try to game me in my courtroom, you will lose!"

I kept my voice steady. "I hear your concerns, Mr. Fowler. And I will not lie to you or try to game you. But here's a word of advice back at you. You can talk. And I promise I'll listen. I'll really listen. But now...here's the important part...I'll listen *up to a point*."

"When do we get to that point?" he asked, calmer now.

"When I say so," I said, taking a chance with my answer. It was actually not my call when negotiations would be broken off and an assault authorized. But I wanted Fowler to believe that I had that power. I wanted him to believe that he was talking directly to the man in charge.

A silence, and then Fowler spoke again.

"Okay, Alex Cross. We've got the start of a deal," Fowler said. "You're going to be my jury foreman."

14

BEFORE I COULD REPLY TO THAT, FOWLER APPARENTLY PULLED THE PHONE AWAY from his mouth because he sounded farther off as he began to scream, "I swear, this snot-nosed kid better shut up, Diana. *Shut her up! Now!*"

I could hear Chloe crying hysterically. I could also hear Diana Fowler Nicholson saying, "Henry, for God's sake, she's scared, she's tired, she's hungry."

Without missing a beat, and with cold sarcasm in his voice, Fowler said, "If she's hungry, tell her to eat the sandwich I brought." Then he let go with a sickening snicker. "PB and J, little Trey's favorite. Don't worry, I'll save him one."

Diana again. "Henry—"

"Shut the hell up, *Diana!*" Fowler screamed. "I have no reason and, frankly, no desire to talk to you!" Then two gunshots.

In his calm voice, Fowler said, "There goes your precious Ming vase and your cute little Swarovski crystal cigarette box, Diana. I just want you to fully understand the reality now: this room, your life, they are nothing but a great big shooting gallery to—"

Dr. Nicholson's voice cut him off. "What's wrong with you, Fowler? You're nothing but—"

Another gunshot. Sweat was pouring off my brow. Children crying, but no other sounds. Then Fowler returned to his crazy screaming voice. "Listen, you pathetic quack! You're the one I most want to put in the grave. Do you understand that? You're the one I want to kill. Do you understand that?"

There was no answer from the doctor.

Then Fowler screamed, *"Do you understand that, Barry?"*

"Listen to him, Barry. Please listen," Diana begged.

"I'm listening," said the doctor, barely audibly. "And of course I understand."

Now Fowler spoke with quiet and controlled rage. "No one in this room should have anything to say, not anything. Not a word. But that's especially true of you, quackster. So listen to me very carefully. If you say one more word, just one...more...word—if you make any sound at all, even a cough or a hiccup—I'm going to kill you. Nod your head yes if you understand the rules."

I assumed that Dr. Nicholson nodded, because Fowler's voice came back to me as if he were returning to a business call he'd put on hold. "Hey, Cross. Sorry to keep you like that. You know how tough a courtroom can be."

"Right," I said, still not quite understanding the twisted logic he had going. The courtroom. The jury. The Grinch. Then it dawned on me that trying to guide him to some safe resolution of the situation was perhaps not the best way forward, at least not yet. Better to play along with his version of reality, and perhaps use it.

"Mr. Fowler. Seeing how you've named me jury foreman, I was wondering if I could come in the house and observe the proceedings," I said matter-of-factly, going for a kind of could-I-borrow-your-lawnmower style.

Nu and McGoey were looking at me as if I were insane.

15

THERE WAS A LONG PAUSE BEFORE FOWLER SAID, "WHY WOULD YOU WANT TO do that, Cross?"

"Don't jury members learn as much from a witness's facial expressions and body language as they do from his testimony?"

Another pause. That pause stretched into thirty seconds. The thirty seconds stretched into the longest minute of my life.

My fear was that Fowler would explode again and turn his guns on the hostages. I could see McGoey shaking his head as if he knew I'd made the wrong move.

Finally Fowler said, "I don't think so, Cross. Nice try, but I don't think so."

Persistence. Persistence.

"It would give me the opportunity to hear your side of the story," I said. "Face-to-face. Man-to-man."

Another few seconds.

Then Fowler said, very quietly, very calmly, "I will frisk you when you come in, Cross. If I find you're carrying a gun, I'm going to kill you. And then I'll kill a hostage or two. Starting with the good Dr. Quack N. Cash."

"I don't need a gun to have a conversation," I said, and I handed my Glock to McGoey.

Fifteen seconds passed. Then Fowler's voice came again.

"Jeremy, go open the front door for Mr. Cross. I'm going to be right behind you, buddy. So don't even think about running out of the house. Understand? Okay, get going." I guess the boy didn't go fast enough, because I heard this father, on Christmas Eve, shout at his eleven-year-old-son, "Move, Jeremy, or I will kick your fucking obscenely obese ass until you do!"

I looked at my watch. It was almost midnight when I got my jacket and hat and headed toward the Nicholsons' house.

I walked through the now empty shelter and out into the falling snow thinking that I should have been with my family right then, at St. Anthony's, singing "O Little Town of Bethlehem" to start midnight mass.

16

WHILE I'D BEEN ON THE PHONE WITH FOWLER, NU AND MCGOEY HAD BEEN putting the storm-and-protect operation into full effect. As I crossed Thirtieth Street I saw that SWAT officers had started circling the house again. Only this time their weapons were cocked and cradled. They were ready for trouble, for anything that might happen in the next few minutes. Like me getting killed.

The second and third floors of the surrounding houses were manned with sharpshooters. Inside those four houses, lights flickered on and off slowly.

Signals were being exchanged. I couldn't begin to work out what they meant. I had other problems to figure out, and figure out fast. In a few seconds I was directly facing the house. My eyes darted to the right and I saw police officers quickly herding reporters back and away. The cops didn't have to ask them twice, which made me wonder if I was making the right move here.

The snow soaked the hem of my pants as I walked the short path to the house. The big front door, flanked by frosted-glass windows, was ajar. From inside the house came the sound of Diana Nicholson weeping. Suddenly, lights were turned off—front rooms, hallway, and all outdoor lights. Total blackout.

I swallowed, stepped up onto the brick entry. The front door swung all the way open. A dark center hall loomed straight ahead. Then I saw the figure of a fat little boy run through the darkness, sobbing, and disappear toward the right.

The night was so quiet that for one crazy moment I thought I could hear snowflakes landing. I stepped into the front hallway. The door shut, and I immediately heard Fowler behind me, breathing heavily.

"Merry Christmas, Cross," he said, and turned on the lights, revealing velvet-flocked wallpaper, really expensive stuff, on both sides of the hall.

"Same to you, Mr. Fowler," I said.

"Hands on the wall," he said. "You know the drill." He cackled. "Always have wanted to say that to a cop."

I said nothing, just put my hands on the wall and spread my legs.

"Hope I didn't make a mistake letting you into the house," Fowler said.

"Well, that makes two of us," I said before I felt the cold steel of a pistol muzzle pressed against the back of my neck.

17

FOWLER DID A DAMN NEAR PROFESSIONAL JOB OF FRISKING ME. PROBABLY because he himself had been the subject of a body search at least thirty times in the last few years. The gun came away from the back of my neck.

"Fingers laced behind your head," he said. "Then walk, and turn right at the end of the hall. If I see your fingers slip or get any sense you're trying to turn on me, I'll shoot first, Cross, and ask no questions later."

I took the man at his word, put my hands where he wanted them, and walked to where his son had disappeared.

"There's an overstuffed chair on your immediate right," Fowler said. "Sit in it, hands on your lap."

It looked like someone had fought a small war in the living room. A large Christmas tree was on its side, branches crushed or snapped by buckshot, its ornaments shattered, its lights out. The debris from the earlier shoot-up of the gifts was everywhere, the remnants almost unrecognizable: pieces of metal from the iPad, bits of gold from whatever Nicholson had had wrapped in the Tiffany box.

To my dismay, the window curtains had all been drawn. No one from the outside could see me, Fowler, or the three children and three adults lying on their bellies on the floor beside the ruins of the Christmas tree. I could feel the pleading hope and fear in their eyes, eyes that were red from fatigue and tension and crying.

An extremely attractive, fit, country-club kind of woman, Diana Nicholson wore only jeans and a black jogging bra. I had no idea what that was about. Her new husband was a big handsome guy who looked like he'd just walked off a sailboat. Everything about him screamed wealth and privilege except for his green-and-red Christmas sweater, which was slit down the back, nearly in two pieces.

I had no idea what that was about either.

The congressman's wife, Melissa Brandywine, was lying next to Nicholson and his wife. A society-page regular, she had copper-colored hair that looked as if it'd just been styled at the salon. Her makeup was flawless too. But she was shaking uncontrollably, as if she were freezing. Why had Fowler involved her? Was it on purpose? Or had she just blundered into the crisis?

The children were an even sorrier sight than the grown-ups, maybe because they were kids in their pajamas and it was Christmas and their innocence had been destroyed. Young Trey was sucking his thumb. Chloe hugged a throw pillow that featured holly, red ribbons, and bells. Her twin, Jeremy, stared at nothing. I saw a dark stain on his pajama pants and realized the poor kid had been so frightened and humiliated by his father that he'd peed his pants.

So I already hated Fowler when he came around in front of me and showed me just how far he'd fallen since his glory days on K Street and in the courtroom. In place of the Italian suits he'd favored, he wore filthy jeans and a torn army-surplus jacket. He'd lost fifty or sixty pounds since those days. His eyes were sunken in his head. Several of his teeth were missing. There were scabs on his face that had been picked at and oozed. He carried a Glock 19 and a Remington shotgun that had been crudely sawed off.

Fowler stared at me for an uncomfortable few seconds, then he smiled, really showing off the rotting gaps where his teeth had been.

"You have time for a joke, Cross?" he asked. "Lighten things up a bit? Holiday spirit and all that?"

18

I WAS BEGINNING TO FEEL IT, THE TURMOIL FOWLER SEEMED TO SECRETE FROM every pore. I could smell it too. He reeked of that weird sour body odor that follows crazy people who live on the street too long.

"So there's this ignorant, oblivious man," Fowler began. "He's sitting on the veranda of his rented bungalow in St. John's with his trophy wife. Beautiful sunset. Glowing tans. They're drinking from a marvelous bottle of burgundy grand cru from the Côte d'Or. His wife says, 'I love you.' The man looks over and says, 'Is that you talking, or is it the wine?' She looks at him as if he's a fool and says, 'Actually, dear, I was talking to the wine.'"

Fowler looked around the room. Nobody was laughing. If anything, they were all even more terrified than before he'd told his joke.

"You remember that, don't you, Diana?" Fowler asked.

"No, Henry, I don't," she said.

He smiled in a threatening way. "Of course you do. And if you don't, you should. It's so emblematic of who we were that—"

"Stop it!" Diana screamed. "You've got to stop this, Henry. At least let the children go."

"Don't be a party pooper, Diana. Show the spirit of the season," Fowler said, waving her off before looking at me. "My dear ex-wife has never dealt well with reality or the truth. As you shall hear, Cross."

I couldn't let this go any further. "She's right, Henry. Why don't you let your children go? It's Christmas, a hard time. But don't take it out on them."

He leveled the pistol at me. "Why shouldn't I take it out on them, Cross? They're the ones who drove me here. They and their uncaring, greedy, materialistic mother, the biggest mistake of my life."

"Mister." I heard a child's voice. It was Trey. He was looking at me. "Mister, can you ask Daddy to go back to his house so Santa can come?"

Before I could deliver any words of comfort, Fowler walked over and jammed his black-booted foot on the boy's ear.

"Shut up, Trey, or we'll be playing Hide the Skippy Super Chunk. Besides, I told you. I'm going no place."

Fowler looked at me, scratched at his face, said, "Kids. They never listen."

I'd begun to compile a catalog of Fowler's tics and twitches—the face scratching, the hand rubbing, the massaging of the back of his neck, the quick bite to the side of his ring finger on his left hand. If he sat next to you on the Metro, you'd stand up quickly, move away, and get off at the next station.

He picked up the phone on the end table next to my chair and hit Redial.

I heard a voice say, "This is Ramiro."

Fowler laid the receiver on the table.

"It's Cross," I said. "I'm all right."

"Now that the jury has been seated, are we ready to hear opening statements?" Fowler said, looking at me.

I hesitated, then nodded.

"Excellent," Fowler said, rubbing the back of his gun hand. "Let's begin with an introduction. Diana, sweetheart? Kids? Barry? This is the famous Alex Cross. He'll be the jury foreman for these proceedings."

His words had lost their frantic quality and now flowed with the easy delivery of a top-flight defense attorney. Despite all the drugs and self-abuse, this madman had polish and brains, which made him even scarier to me.

"Court is now in session!" Fowler intoned in a deep voice, as if he were a bailiff. "The Honorable Grinch Who Stole Christmas presiding!"

19

FOWLER BEGAN MARCHING AROUND THE ROOM SINGING AT THE TOP OF HIS lungs, *"He's a mean one, Mr. Grinch!"* Then he stopped next to his ex-wife and put his boot on her back.

"First up in the box," Fowler said, looking at me. "The evil mastermind behind my destruction: Diana Alstead Fowler Nicholson."

"Henry," she said and began to whimper.

"Hush now, Diana," Fowler soothed. "I'll talk for you. If I get anything wrong, you just speak up." He looked up. "The fair Diana Alstead was originally from Charleston, South Carolina. Daughter of parents born into multigenerational wealth, she grew up in a life of ease, the expectation of immediate material gratification simply a part of her DNA. She attended the finest schools, Choate Rosemary Hall and then Georgetown. There she meets this kid on full scholarship. Henry

Fowler is beneath her station in life, but he shows promise. He's majoring in chemistry and English and wins entry to the Georgetown law school. She sees he's a hardworking guy and latches onto him like a leech in a swamp."

Diana was looking at me with this pitiful expression as she cried, "That's not true, Henry. I loved you."

"Oh, boo-hoo, Cindy Lou Who. We're telling the truth here, not repeating old fantasies," Fowler said. "I had almost twenty years to study this particular specimen, Mr. Foreman. Here is my expert testimony: Diana is that woman at the Sotheby's jade auction bidding far too much for a ten-thousand-dollar green statue of a water buffalo, or a yak, I'm not sure which. She's that woman who sets her authentic Regency dining table with two-thousand-dollar James Robinson place settings. She's the type they fawn over at Bloomies and Bergdorf Goodman, the woman whose skinny little ass they kiss at Prada, the woman they serve tea to in private rooms at Tiffany in Washington *and* New York. Yes, my ex is quite the gal.

"Hey, she shared her genes with me to create this winning trio," he said, gesturing to his children.

"You've already met Trey, who's never met an allergy or affliction he didn't adore. Sick all the time, right from birth, pneumonia then. You name a childhood disease, and my boy's had it. Meets with top medical specialists two, three times a week. Best that money can buy, isn't that right, son?"

Trey began to snivel. "I can't help it, Dad."

"Of course you can't," Fowler said soothingly. "Most

of your mother's defective DNA strands just happened to spool out to you. And those that didn't found their way into your older brother and sister."

He smiled at me. "I'm a lucky, lucky man, Cross."

"That so?" I asked, hoping he'd continue to vent, expend his emotional energy, and then see the hopelessness of his situation before the meth could turn him full rhino.

"Isn't it obvious?" Fowler asked acidly. "Doesn't luck just seem to shimmer all around me?"

"It used to," I said.

He looked off into the distance, said, "Yes, it did, before my surroundings and close companions conspired to warp me."

Here was paranoia, crystal meth's staple emotion. I could already hear the angry persecution story coming.

Fowler didn't let me down.

20

FOWLER CROSSED TO HIS SON JEREMY AND USED HIS BOOT TO PUSH THE BOY over onto his back, where he cringed like a dog.

"Here he is," Fowler said. "My scion. The apple of my eye. Make that the apple strudel, cake, pie, and Pop-Tart of my eye. Not to mention my favorite bed wetter. By the looks of it, he's regressing, pissing his pants now, instead of his mattress."

The boy was humiliated. Jeremy began to make hiccupping noises that broke into chokes and sobs.

"Stop, Daddy!" Chloe screamed. "You're making it worse. You're ruining everything! You always ruin everything!"

"Ahh, Chloe," Fowler said. "My Little Miss Perfect." He looked to me. "Chloe is exceptionally smart, a trait that no doubt came from my end of things. But that intelligence crossed with my ex-wife's narcissism produced a young lady who tries to control the world as if it orbited around her head."

"I get it, Henry," I said. "Your kids didn't turn out the way you planned. Welcome to the club. It's what makes them human. And the disappointment? That's your issue. Deal with it."

He looked surprised, then his eyes narrowed and he snarled, "Who the fuck do you think you are, Dr. Phil?"

"Isn't that why you asked me in here?" I said.

"I asked you in to serve as jury foreman," he snapped. "I'm running the show here, or haven't you noticed?"

"Look," I said. "It's Christmas Eve. You obviously aren't happy with your life or your family. But I am happy. I have a family I love. I'd like to get back to them, so I'd appreciate it if you'd tell me what it was that broke you."

Fowler didn't know what to make of that. He clearly hadn't expected it.

"What are you talking about?" he demanded.

"You were at the top of the game on K Street, making millions, making headlines, and then it all unravels," I said. "I get the overspending, the consumerist wife, the messed-up kids. But lots of guys in this town have those problems, and they aren't holding their families hostage on Christmas Eve. So what was it? What caused you to unravel?"

21

FOR A SECOND THERE I WONDERED IF I'D GONE TOO FAR, BEEN TOO DIRECT, TOO confrontational. But then Fowler smiled icily at me.

"You want to know the straw that broke the camel's back, Cross?" he asked, reaching into his jacket and coming up with a glass vial.

"Wouldn't hurt to understand your side of things," I said.

Fowler squatted by the glass coffee table, tapped white powder onto it, and started laying the powder out in lines with a hotel-room key card. "I suppose that's a reasonable request, but I'm going to have to get my head on straight to tell that story."

He rolled up a dollar bill and snorted two of the five lines. Shuddering, he closed his eyes, then he shivered and said, "Now, that's more like it."

"How long have you been up, Henry?" I asked.

"It doesn't matter," he said. "I'm seeing things clear and for what they are, Cross. So I'll tell you what you want to know about me going off the deep end."

"Okay," I said, noticing the slight tremor that was visible in his fingers. If he had been shooting and snorting meth for more than, say, thirty-six hours, the rhino could be paying us a visit at any moment.

"So it's Christmas not that many years ago," Fowler began. "And we're home. We're happy. We hold a party the afternoon of Christmas Eve. It's been a big-money year for me, and Diana's spared no expense. Catered. The whole nine yards. And I don't know why, but it was one of those years when people stayed in DC for the holidays. Nearly everyone we knew came. Even Barry, an old friend from Georgetown, who arrived dressed as Santa Claus. Even dear Melissa and her husband, Congressman Brandywine, made an appearance. Anyway, about an hour into the festivities, I'm working the room. A potential client asks for a business card and I go to my office. Door's locked. I knock. No one answers."

Fowler paused, snorted two more lines, then got to his feet and shrugged. "Locked door. It happens. I'll get it open later. But anyway, long story short, I go back to the party, apologize to my potential client, and promise to contact him after the New Year. I get a drink. I'm looking around. The party's right at its peak. I get this weird feeling. So I go out the back door and around to the bulkhead below my office window. I look in and what do I see?"

Fowler walked over to stand by Dr. Nicholson. Then

he booted the man hard in the ribs. Over the doctor's groaning, Fowler said, "This one's sitting in my Georgetown law school rocking chair. Dear Diana, my lovely wife of many years, is kneeling before him, and—" He broke into song. "'I saw Mommy sucking Santa Claus, underneath the mistletoe so bright!'"

22

DIANA HAD TURNED BEET RED AND WOULD NOT MEET MY EYES. DR. NICHOLSON was still crunched up after the kick to his ribs.

"Says a lot, that you loved her so much that seeing her with another man would crush you like that," I told Fowler. "But is that true?"

Fowler looked at me with instant hatred. "You calling me a liar, Cross?" He pointed to his wife. "I didn't confront her. I wanted to know how deep this went, whether he was a fling or something more. Turns out she was fucking the eyeglass maker like he was the featured artist in the stud-of-the-month club. Can you believe it? She was pissing away our marriage with a guy who makes a living by saying, 'Now, can you read the next line? What about the line under that?'"

He glared at his ex-wife and Barry, and I feared he'd start kicking them again, or worse. Fowler shook the pistol at Dr. Nicholson and said to me, "They had a standing reservation for a room at the Four Seasons, where they'd screw their brains out and stick me with the tab." Fowler's face had turned bright red. He paced the room, nervously scratching his arms and chest.

"Are you beginning to understand what happened here, Cross? What drove me to debase myself? Do you see who the victim is now?"

I said nothing. I just looked at Fowler and tried to seem objective. There would be no stopping his rant. He pointed to Melissa Brandywine.

"Now, you may be wondering who this lucky holiday guest is. Well, show Mr. Cross your pretty face, Missy. I said show him your face." He grabbed her by the chin and squeezed hard.

She cried out. "Henry, please."

"C'mon, Missy, show the big phony smile that helped get your husband elected to Congress. While you're at it, show him your net-worth statement, and Cross will understand why your husband really got elected to Congress."

The congressman's wife turned her head toward me. She looked sad, broken, and embarrassed, and I had to wonder why.

"Dear Mrs. Brandywine," Fowler said. "The publicity expert. The woman behind all those White House luncheons and all those embassy receptions. You know who else she is?"

"Henry, please don't," Melissa Brandywine said.

"Nonsense," Fowler said. "It's time to lay all our cards

on the table. Not even dear Diana knows this, but after discovering that my wife was a whore, I got drunk and decided *I* deserved a whore. And who better to turn to than the wife of a man whore? She'd made overtures before. I just decided to take her up on it. Little secret? She likes a finger up the—"

Diana screamed, "The children! Henry! *Your children, for God's sake!* Why can't you stop this? Why can't you move on? Why do you have to destroy everything around you? Just let it go."

To my astonishment, Fowler did not explode. He just stood there looking like he'd come to in the middle of a sleepwalk. Everything was suddenly quiet in the room, so eerily quiet that I thought I could hear snowflakes against the windows behind the thick curtains.

Fowler walked quickly to a sofa that faced the hostages. He sat down, waved the gun slowly at them, and said as if in a trance, "I want to let it go, Diana, but it won't let me go."

He looked at me. "Ever feel like that, Cross? That something just won't let you go?"

I flashed on the dark shadow fleeing the scene as my first wife lay dying in my arms. "Sure."

"Then you'll understand that it's time for you to go," he said. "The trial's over. All have been found guilty, and I've got a penalty phase to prepare for."

23

"DON'T DO THIS," I SAID. "NO MATTER WHAT TRUST MAY HAVE BEEN BROKEN. No matter what was done to you, Fowler, this is not the way to deal with it."

His eyes flashed. "That's not for you to decide. Now, get out before I start thinking it's a good idea to finish you off too. Go back to that family you love, Cross. And pity mine."

I could see by the flat quality of his expression and eyes that I did not have much room to negotiate. Standing slowly, I said, "I appreciate your side of things, Henry."

"And I appreciate you listening, Mr. Foreman," Fowler said.

"Can I take one of them with me?" I asked, motioning toward his hostages. "A gesture of goodwill?"

"Leave."

"Show me you're willing to compromise," I said, backing out of the room. "Otherwise you limit my options, Henry. You force my hand, make me inclined to take harsher measures."

"I don't care, Cross," he said. "Threats work only on men who are scared for their lives, and I lost mine a long, long time ago."

"Henry—"

He pointed the pistol at me. "Leave or *you* die right now."

"I can't believe you want to kill them," I said.

"You don't, huh?" he said, and marched up to Dr. Nicholson, who cowered as if he expected to be kicked again.

Fowler glared at me with an I-told-you-so expression, extended his arm, looked back at his ex-wife's husband, aimed the gun, and shot him.

CHAPTER

24

NICHOLSON BUCKED, AND THEN HE SAGGED, AND HIS BRIGHT HOLIDAY SWEATER turned into a sponge for the blood seeping out of him. With the gunshot still ringing in my ears, I grabbed a sofa throw pillow and moved straight at Nicholson. His wife beat me to him.

"Barry!" she screamed. "Barry?"

I went to my knees, tried to lift his sweater and shirt to see the extent of his injuries.

"Get the hell away from him, Diana!" Fowler yelled. "Don't you dare help him. You never helped me when I was hurting."

Diana screeched, "You filthy, insane animal!"

Jeremy, Chloe, and Trey were sobbing. Melissa Brandywine was up on her hands and knees dry-heaving.

I was still trying to see the wound.

There's no such thing as a good bullet wound, but a

gut wound is particularly bad. It can kill in a few minutes or a few hours. A bullet might rupture the colon, for example, or the liver. Fecal matter could splatter in the system and cause a bacterial infection that won't stop. Bones could shatter into the kidneys, into the spleen, causing a swifter death. In any case, we had to believe the man was a mess inside and needed a doctor now.

"I said to get the hell away from him!" Fowler shouted again. "I mean it!"

I thought it would be a matter of seconds before he put a bullet into Diana, or me, or both of us. Then she stood up, her eyes blazing. "Go ahead, then!" she shrieked. "It's what you want, Henry. Go ahead and kill me. But let the rest of them go. Let Cross take Barry and the children and Melissa out of here, and then you can do to me whatever it is you think I deserve."

"No," Fowler said. "Barry's not going anywhere. And neither are you."

She pivoted and crouched beside me. "What can we do?"

I could see the entry wound now. It was to the far right of the navel, close to the side of Nicholson's torso. That was good news and made me wonder whether Fowler's point-blank shot had been intentionally bad.

But then I rolled the eye doctor onto his side, saw that the exit wound was draining blood. A puddle of it already stained the carpet.

I rammed the sofa pillow against the wound, took off my belt, and strapped it in place. "You've got to get some alcohol into the wound," I said.

"Get out, Cross!" Fowler screamed. "Now, or you'll never see Christmas morning or your family again."

I felt the gun barrel against the back of my head. "I'm sorry," I said.

Tears dribbled down Diana's cheeks. "I am too."

I got up, took one last glance around so I could describe the room and everyone's position in it, then turned and walked to the front door. Fowler followed me, about ten feet behind. I unlocked the door and started to open it, wondering whether Fowler intended to shoot me in the back of the head as I left.

25

I STEPPED OUT INTO BRILLIANT, BLINDING LIGHT AND JUMPED WHEN FOWLER slammed the door after me. I stood there a moment, hands on my thighs, trying to get control of my breathing, trying to focus on something other than the wounded doctor and the five other hostages I'd left inside with a madman.

"Alex!" I heard Adam Nu yell. "Move!"

I snapped to alertness and started through the snow, toward the lights. Shortly before midnight, it had been a little above my ankles. Nearly two hours later, the snow was well up my shins and falling faster than I'd ever seen in Washington, two, maybe three inches an hour. Rocky Mountain rates.

The farther I got from the house, the more satellite trucks I could see. This was clearly the media event of a slow news day. But, hey, what was Christmas without a hostage crisis? It was a tradition, just like the mandatory car bomb in Bethlehem.

There were also folks from the neighborhood out, which surprised me. There were even some kids. Shouldn't they all be sleeping? Several folks had camera phones held high above their heads. They clicked. They texted. They Tweeted.

But it was the MPD people who blew me away. There must have been fifty rank-and-file officers now at the scene. They held pistols and four-foot-high shields, and they waited for me. I thought I heard something behind me, but I did not turn. A voice from the crowd called, "Merry Christmas, Detective!"; it was followed by a smattering of applause and a few whistles.

Then I heard a woman's voice—coming from close *behind me.*

"Mr. Cross," she said. "Detective, please wait."

I spun around. The congressman's wife was staggering through the snow toward me in her stocking feet, sad, stunned, still shaking like a leaf. She was carrying a shovel. I went to her, lifted her out of the snow, and carried her through the line of policemen in riot gear.

"What's with the shovel?" I asked as I handed her over to a pair of EMTs inside the shelter behind the police vans.

She looked at me in bewilderment. "He said it was for you. That you were to keep the front walk clear of snow if you wanted to see any more of the hostages alive." Then she began to cry. "Mr. Cross?"

"Yes, Mrs. Brandywine?"

She shivered beneath the blanket the EMTs had wrapped her in and wouldn't meet my gaze but said, "You won't be repeating... the things he said?"

"No, ma'am," I replied. "I'm not in the habit of quoting madmen."

The congressman's wife nodded, her lower lip trembling. "Thank you."

"It's got to be a decent Christmas for someone. It might as well be you."

Book Two
THE YULETIDE MERRY

26

"WELL, LOOK WHO GOT OUT IN ONE PIECE," SAID ADAM NU, WHO CAME IN from the storm as the medics moved Mrs. Brandywine to an ambulance. Then Nu gave me a quick hug, which wasn't like him at all.

I let out a breath. "Yeah, it wasn't a lot of fun. But if I don't get some hot coffee and food, I'm going to be useless."

One of Nu's men got me a ham sandwich and a steaming Styrofoam cup of French roast, a holiday feast that I wolfed down as I stood by the gas heater. Then I asked, "What did you hear over the phone?"

"Some of it," McGoey said. "When he was yelling or singing or you were talking. Guy's a barking lunatic."

"He is, but I don't see him executing the family," I said.

"You said he shot Nicholson," Nu said.

"He did," I replied. "But not to kill. He was at point-blank range. He could easily have made a shot that was guaranteed to turn Nicholson's lights out."

"Maybe he wants him to suffer," Nu said.

"Or doesn't believe himself a killer deep down," I replied. "He did let Mrs. Brandywine go, and it could be an indicator of his willingness to negotiate an ending to this without further bloodshed."

"Sorry to spoil the holiday," McGoey said. "But you've got Fowler all wrong, Alex."

"How's that?" I asked, annoyed that he was trying to tell me about a man he'd never met.

He got out his cell phone and said, "Remember before you went in, we talked about the skank meth addict Fowler lived with?"

"Patty something," I said.

"Patty Paradise, aka Patricia Kocot," McGoey said. "I had someone go to her crib, see if she'd be willing to come down and talk some sense into her boy."

"And?"

The detective got a laptop and showed me the most recent picture of Patty Paradise. She was naked, slumped in a bathtub. She had two bullet holes in her forehead, and split skin and angry bruising along her forearms and shins, clear indications she'd been electrocuted before being shot.

27

AS NU AND HIS MEN PREPARED AN ASSAULT PLAN BASED ON WHAT I'D TOLD them about the layout of the house and the position of the hostages, Ramiro and other officers began calling the Nicholson residence again, trying to make a connection with Henry Fowler once more.

Despite the coffee and the food, I was suddenly exhausted. I told McGoey I was going to catch a catnap but to wake me if Fowler answered. The van was equipped with two bunks that folded down off the wall. I grabbed a blanket, lay down, and closed my eyes.

I've always been one of those people who can fall asleep at a moment's notice. It's a skill that's handy when you're involved with this kind of drawn-out fiasco. But that night I couldn't fall asleep. Not at first, at least.

My brain kept replaying what Fowler had said and done; I tried to use what he'd told me to connect the man he had been with the animal he was now.

I don't believe him, I thought as I finally drifted off to sleep. *There's something going on here that we're not seeing.*

CHAPTER

28

NOBODY AT THE CROSSES' GETS UP EARLIER THAN NANA. NOT EVEN ON Christmas.

That morning she rose at a quarter to five.

First thing she did was dial up the thermostat in the house and "put up the coffee," as she liked to say. Then she turned on the lights on the tree, brought a big CVS shopping bag into the living room, and got started on the stockings. Filling the stockings was her job. She enjoyed it immensely. And everybody seemed to like the candy and the dollar-store goodies as much as the pricier shirts and sweaters and books and electronic games.

Nana doled out the tiny plastic puzzles and Hershey bars and ballpoint pens. As always, each of the stocking gifts had a double meaning. She gave Bree a disposable lighter; it was Nana's way of telling her that she knew Bree sneaked an occasional cigarette.

The old woman put a bottle of OPI nail polish in Ava's stocking, thinking it might inspire the girl to stop biting her nails.

She dropped iPod earbuds into Damon's stocking. A bright red hair clip went into Jannie's. And the one-handed flosser was for Alex.

"Alex," she said softly. She looked out the front window. It was still coming down and snow was piled more than a foot high on the cars. But there was no sign of her grandson.

"My, my," she heard someone say. "Santa's helpers get younger and prettier every year."

Nana turned around and saw Bree standing at the edge of the living room. They hugged and wished each other a merry Christmas, both of them knowing it wasn't all that merry without Alex in the house.

"Did you get any sleep?" Nana asked.

"Not a wink."

"Makes two of us," Nana said. "Terrible knot in my stomach all night."

They drank coffee and kept each other company. Jannie and Damon and Ava joined them just as Christmas Day was dawning. Everyone smiled and hugged and said merry Christmas, but the usual rush to rip open gifts just wasn't there.

"What this Christmas morning needs is a good hot breakfast," Nana said.

They all pretended to agree with her.

"Well, let's get into the kitchen and get to work. You don't think I'm going to fix it all by myself, do you?" said Nana. "I need helpers."

The children followed her into the kitchen. Bree said she'd join them in a minute. "I love cracking eggs. Save that job for me," she called after them.

Then she picked up the remote and flicked on the television. Words at the bottom of the screen said CHRISTMAS HOSTAGE CRISIS.

There was a shot of the big, handsome house in Georgetown. Snow and people and cops were everywhere. Then there was Alex carrying a woman from the house where the lunatic had been holed up. The news anchor identified her as Congressman Brandywine's wife and said, "Detective Cross risked his life and entered the house unarmed to negotiate face-to-face with the madman. One life has been saved, but from what we understand, another one hangs in the balance—Fowler shot and wounded his ex-wife's husband."

He'd gone into the house unarmed. Someone had been shot inside. Bree thought about that and said softly, as if the TV could hear her, "Oh, Alex, Alex, Alex. I don't know if I can bear where you go."

Then she changed the channel.

But Channel 4 had the identical story. That network, however, had a reporter on the scene. She held a microphone and was talking to the camera.

"From superlawyer to drug addict to madman: that's the road Henry Fowler took to arrive here this Christmas morning—"

Bree punched POWER, threw the remote down. She rubbed her sleeve against her damp eyes. Then she shouted toward the kitchen, "Nobody better have touched those eggs!"

I FELT SOMEONE SHAKING ME. I JERKED AWAKE AND WAS SURPRISED TO SEE Detective McGoey standing in a weak, pale light.

"It's Fowler," he said. "A couple of minutes ago it sounded like he was going rhino in there, and Nu was getting ready to give his men the go to assault when Fowler answered the phone, finally. He's asking for you, Alex."

I nodded, sat up, shook the cobwebs from my head. "Time is it?"

"Six fifteen," McGoey said.

"I slept for four hours?" I said.

"There was no reason to wake you until now," he said.

I nodded dumbly, followed him toward the front of the van and Ramiro, who held out a phone to me. "This is Cross," I said.

"I'm disappointed in you" announced Fowler's voice. "Very disappointed."

"Why?"

"You betrayed me. I've been looking out my windows. You've got me surrounded by an army."

"That's the way it usually works when you're armed to the teeth and you don't talk to us," I said.

"Are they coming in after me? Are they going to shoot their way in?"

"Unless you talk to us."

"Coming in here would be a mistake," he said. "All you would find are bodies around the Christmas tree, mine included."

"But you'll talk to me?" I asked. "Help me try to figure out a way to avoid that?"

He didn't reply, but he didn't hang up either.

"Is Dr. Nicholson still alive?" I asked.

"Barry?" he shot back. "Sure, he's alive. But he's got a hell of a stomachache."

"Let him go," I said. "Let me come in there with another unarmed officer and get him."

"No," Fowler said. "I'm enjoying his suffering."

"Then let someone else in there go. One of your children."

Silence, and then he said, "A goodwill gesture, isn't that what you said it would be?"

"That's right."

"Wish granted," he said. "I'm sending out the only one in this house I really care about."

Nu knocked on the wall, signaled me toward the van's

side window. I got up, saw the front door open. A black Labrador retriever with a red bow around its neck slunk out, and it startled and began to run away, its tail between its legs, when the door slammed shut.

30

FOWLER WAS DEFINITELY TOYING WITH US, DEMONSTRATING THAT EVEN WHEN HE was in mortal danger, with threats from the snipers and SWAT assaulters all around him, he was the one who decided who lived, who died. I could have gone the anger route, called him on it, put more pressure on him, but something told me it would backfire.

"You love your dog, Fowler?" I asked.

"What kind of man doesn't love his dog?" he replied sharply.

"A man who has a cat," I said.

"Funny, Cross."

"I appreciate you letting the dog go," I said. "What's the dog's name?"

"Mindy," Fowler said.

"We thank you for releasing Mindy, and I assure you she'll be well cared for. But I need more, Fowler, if I'm going to keep these trained professionals from kicking down your door and trying to blow your head off before you can hurt anyone else."

A long silence. "Like what?"

I looked over at Nu and McGoey and then said, "I want to come in again—with medical personnel. I want to take Barry out of there."

Fowler began to scream, finally going rhino. We heard things breaking, and then he came back on the line. "I don't care what you want! I want what I want! Barry's going to die! Got that? He's going to die for what he did to me! And so is my ex-wife. They took my life! Now I'm going to take theirs. I am going to kill them all."

"I'm coming in, Henry," I said. "Right now."

But he'd hung up.

31

"PANCAKES OR WAFFLES?" NANA ASKED IN A VOICE SO CHEERFUL THAT everybody knew it was put on. Add to that the fact that both Jannie (always pro-waffle) and Damon (fiercely pro-pancake) said they didn't really care, and it was obvious that worry about Alex had pretty much sucked the joy right out of the holiday.

"It's Christmas," Nana finally said. "Why don't I just make both? Pancakes *and* waffles coming up!"

No response from the kids.

Suddenly Nana yanked off her apron and flung it to the kitchen floor. "Enough of this!" she shouted and began to march up and down, swinging her fists like she was punching the heavy bag in the basement.

That got everyone's attention.

"Now, you all listen to me," Nana said, snatching up a wooden mixing spoon and shaking it at them. "I don't like this terrible situation any more than you do. I've got a grandson who's missing for Christmas. Does it make me gloomy? Does it make me angry? Does it make me sad?"

She peered around at them in the intimidating way she'd perfected as a vice principal. "The answer to all three of those questions is yes. It certainly does. My heart's as heavy as yours. I could burst into tears any minute. Fact is, I did, twice last night, and I may do it again. But the truth is, life has to be lived. *This* Christmas is today. Now. *This* Christmas will never come again. And I don't mean to be giving a holiday sermon, but Christmas is about hope and faith. And we'd all better realize that, you hear me? Hope and faith. You hear me?"

Except for bacon popping in the frying pan, the room was silent.

"I said—*you hear me?*"

"It's hard to feel hope and faith when you're sick to your stomach," said Jannie. "No one who doesn't live in a police family can understand what this feels like, Nana."

"It sucks," Damon added.

"I don't disagree with any of that," their great-grandmother said. "If it were easy, I wouldn't have to be delivering this lecture."

"Okay, we embrace hope and faith," Bree said. She squeezed Nana's shoulders and gave her a kiss. "At least, I do."

"Now, that's fine," Nana said. "I hope your stepchildren will have the same common sense. Now, whoever dropped my apron on the floor, please pick it up and give it to me."

Everyone laughed...a little.

"Then we'll have a real fine breakfast," she went on. "And then we'll go into the living room, and we'll each open up one gift. And then..."

"Then what?" Ava asked.

"Then Damon will go out and shovel the front walk. *So when his father gets home we can all go to church.*"

CHAPTER

32

"YOU ARE NOT GOING BACK IN THERE," LIEUTENANT NU SAID. "I'LL NEVER BE able to look your wife in the eye again."

"Join the club on that one," I said, jumping up. "But I've got to go back in there, or that doctor is dead and maybe the others too. And I have a plan."

"And that plan is?" McGoey asked.

I told Nu that while I'd slept, part of my mind must have worked out what was really behind Fowler's fall from glory and his actions of the past twenty-four hours.

"We can use it, I think," I said, and I told them what I was considering.

"Shit," Nu grumbled. "You do have to go back in there."

He hustled me into a SWAT armored vest, and I went back out into the blizzard once more. It was six thirty, a pale winter dawn, the second time I crossed Thirtieth

Street to the Nicholsons' home. The newscasters and on-lookers had been pushed back. Only the vans and the MPD officers, the medics, and the SWAT teams were al-lowed to remain close to the house.

I picked up the shovel the congressman's wife had brought me and started shoveling my way up the walk through thirteen inches of snow. Church bells rang from the direction of O Street, probably Christ Church. From the other direction, more bells, probably Mt. Zion.

More than ever I felt like I was part of something that was staining the celebration, and as I rapped on the front door, I felt ready to do some cleaning up. But was I right? Would my plan work?

I heard the creak of floorboards, and my resolve grew weaker.

The door opened. I stepped inside, hands raised. Fowler kicked shut the door, pushed me face-up against the wall, and frisked me again. "Not a good idea, Cross," he said as he searched me. "Coming back in here."

"Why's that?"

"I can't let you leave now."

33

BECAUSE IT WAS CHRISTMAS MORNING, A SPECIAL DAY, NANA AGREED TO MAKE her sweet bacon. The recipe: thick bacon fried in a cast-iron skillet, then covered with brown sugar and baked in the oven.

"I only cook sweet bacon for a holiday or a birthday," she had always said. That used to be the rule of the house. Her house, she insisted, even though Alex had bought and paid for it. But once, Damon had insisted that Arbor Day was a real holiday, and Nana had agreed with him. And after that, she changed the rule. Now she said: "I only cook sweet bacon for a *major* holiday or a birthday."

Waffles. Pancakes. Cheese grits. And sweet bacon.

"There may be no need to cook the turkey later on," Bree said. "This meal could last me the whole day. Maybe the whole week."

"You speak for yourself," Damon said. "I'll be ready for turkey and mashed potatoes. And those yams I love with the mini-marshmallows."

The maple syrup was soaking into the waffles and pancakes. The sweet bacon strips were crunchy-crisp. And the mood was finally cheerful.

Then Jannie spoke. "You know, it seems to me there's only one thing missing from this breakfast table," she said.

They all immediately thought of Alex. A somber mood reinvaded the room. There was quiet. Nana squeezed her lips together to keep from tearing up. Bree looked out the window of the kitchen door.

Damon shot a why'd-you-make-everyone-feel-bad-again look at Jannie. She realized that her innocent comment had been misinterpreted and had upset everyone.

Jannie said, "Oh, no! Listen. Listen. What I meant was, what's missing are those ridiculous reindeer antlers and the flickering electric red nose that Damon puts on every Christmas."

"Oh, I forgot all about those stupid...those *stunning* antlers," Nana said.

"Get outta here," Damon said. "That's not happening. You wear the antlers. Nana can wear the antlers."

"Nobody wears those antlers like you," Jannie said and giggled.

"Oh please, can I see them on you? Oh *please*," said Ava.

"I don't even know where those dumb things are," Damon said.

"Lucky for us I do," said Jannie. "I've got them right here."

And she produced from under her chair a pair of cloth antlers attached to a headband and decorated with a sprig of plastic holly. She also had a tiny red lightbulb fixed to a big rubber band that would fit snugly around Damon's head.

Then Nana said, "Before we see Damon dressed like a reindeer, let's join hands and say a prayer."

They held hands and bowed their heads. Nana spoke.

"Dear Lord, Who on this blessed Christmas Day brought Your Son into the world, we ask You to look with kindness on another son. Your son Alex. As he strives to help others, we ask You to help him. To keep him from harm. To protect him from evil. According to Your holy will."

Then together the Cross family said, "Amen."

34

STRANGELY, THE SOUNDS I'D COME TO ASSOCIATE WITH THE NICHOLSON HOUSE were gone. No weeping, no screaming, and no children's voices. Even the crazy man who ran the show was silent as he walked behind me, prodding me forward with the muzzle of one of the shotguns.

I surveyed the wreckage of the room in the light that seeped in from behind the curtains. The three children were still lying on the floor and seemed to be sleeping. A red velvet club chair had been viciously slashed open since I left. A mahogany end table had been broken up and the pieces partially burned in the fireplace.

Diana sat cross-legged on the floor with her husband's head resting on her lap. She looked pale and exhausted. The doctor looked a whole lot worse. He lay motionless, his eyes closed. This was a life-or-death situation, and I had a good idea which side of the equation Nicholson was favoring.

I glanced at Fowler, who'd edged around the room but was still covering me with the shotgun. He was less manic than when I'd left him more than four hours before. His eyes were droopy, as if he'd taken something to counteract the methamphetamine, which meant he was vulnerable. That was good; if he almost passed out, it would give me a chance to subdue him. But if he went back to the meth, he'd quickly turn unpredictable.

"Why are you wearing the vest?" he asked, and I thought I smelled liquor.

"My boss made me wear it," I replied as I moved toward Nicholson and his wife. "Said I couldn't come in here without it."

"Means they're coming soon," Fowler said.

"Only if you want it that way, Henry," I said, kneeling next to the wounded doctor to take his pulse. It was slow, erratic, but it was *there*.

"He's dying," Diana whispered. "And there's nothing I can do."

"That's all right," Henry said behind me. "Let them come."

I heard the *tap, tap, tap* of steel on glass, looked over my shoulder, and saw exactly what I did not want to see. Fowler had dumped the rest of his meth in the vial out onto the coffee table.

"That necessary, Henry?" I asked.

"Course," he said, grinning at me maliciously with his rotten teeth. "How else am I going to be alert enough to see all this to its logical conclusion?"

He bent over, booted a line up each nostril. He sat up and shook his head, as if the meth had lit a fire in there. "There you go," he said. "That's how you get the edge on."

"Henry, we've got to get Barry some help."

"You're like everybody else here, Cross," Fowler said, skin flushing as he went into another one of his rages. "*Nobody listens.* Or if they do happen to listen, they don't understand what I'm saying. That was Diana all the way. In one ear and out the other. What I'm saying is *Barry boy's going to die anyway.* We are all going to die anyway. Now, I could plug another bullet into his belly to finish the job, but I want Diana to see him slowly wind down like a goddamned toy. Yeah, a toy. Like that stupid electric poodle that Chloe has. Bark-bark-bark. Then two barks, then one bark, then no bark."

I found myself shaking my head in amazement at his bizarrely directed venom. Diana, however, looked weary and close to collapse. She ignored Fowler's ravings and just kept gently stroking her husband's pale hand.

"Henry, I came in here because I had some questions about the story you told me earlier."

"What story?" he asked.

"Why you're here," I said, getting up. "Why you're doing this."

"I told you everything you needed to know," Fowler sneered.

I looked around, trying to feel my way through uncharted territory and help Nicholson without setting Fowler off. I spotted an unscathed bottle of Absolut vodka on a shelf opposite the downed Christmas tree.

I moved toward it, saying, "But you didn't tell me everything there was to know, did you, Henry?"

"You got all you're going to get," Fowler said as I picked up the bottle. "What are you doing?"

"Helping Barry," I said.

Fowler flicked off the safety on the shotgun. "I told you that was not happening."

"Then I guess you'll have to shoot me," I said, spotting a dress shirt in a gift bag that had been torn open during Fowler's long tirade.

I looked up to see him aiming the shotgun at me. Somehow I stayed calm and said, "But if you shoot me and the rest of your family, no one will ever know what became of you, Henry. You'll be written off as just some lunatic rather than a man who couldn't stomach being himself."

35

SWEAT BROKE OUT ON FOWLER'S BROW, MAKING HIM LOOK GREASY. "WHAT IS that supposed to mean?" he demanded.

I tossed the shirt to the wounded doctor's wife. "Get the straight pins out of this thing. We'll use it as a clean dressing."

"What the hell are you doing, Cross?" he said, jittery. "Just—just what the hell are you doing?"

I turned back to Fowler. "However this turns out, it'll be better for you without a murder charge on your hands. I want to help Barry make it through so that you can atone for what you've done already."

Fowler narrowed eyes that had turned black and beady. "I don't know what you're talking about."

"It's your only hope of redemption," I said, opening the

vodka bottle. "The only thing that you can do that will make this all seem, hell, justifiable."

"All the pins are out of the shirt, Mr. Cross," Diana said. "What now?"

I ignored Fowler and knelt beside her wounded husband. I poured about a cup of the Absolut over and into the entry wound. The sting and burn of the vodka contacting the traumatized area startled the doctor, causing him to groan and come awake for a few seconds.

Nicholson's eyes opened but didn't focus. Diana leaned in closer to him and whispered, "I love you, Barry," before his eyes closed again.

She didn't whisper softly enough. Fowler heard it too, and it destroyed whatever doubt and whatever hope I might have sown in his disturbed mind.

Fowler lifted the shotgun, and fired... right through the ceiling, almost directly over his head. It was deafening, and it made a gaping hole.

"Get away from him right now, Cross, or you're going to have a hole in you."

The phone rang. I grabbed it and shouted: "*No one is hurt! This is Cross.*"

I tossed the phone and returned to Nicholson, hearing Fowler run the pump action on the shotgun. "Who said you could answer the phone?" he said.

"Give me a minute with him, Henry, and then the attention will be right back where you want it. Please?"

I don't know if it was the word *please* or the promise of undivided attention, but something brought Fowler back to a few seconds of sanity.

"Do what you want," he said, returning to the coffee table and the remaining lines of meth. "Take the bullet out with a steak knife and a fork, for all I care."

I poured vodka on my hands, took the shirt from Diana, and ripped it in half. I unbuckled the belt that held the throw pillow to Nicholson's back, and his wife and I rolled him up onto his side so I could pour vodka into the exit wound; I prayed that the alcohol would kill some of the bacteria that had to be spreading in the doctor's abdomen. The pillow was wet with blood as well as a yellowish fluid, which couldn't be good. I hit the area with an extra dose of vodka. Then I drenched the rag, folded it, and pressed it to the wound.

As I did, I heard Fowler snorting the last of his meth. *Good,* I thought. *He'll be about as unbalanced chemically as he can be when I try to really unbalance him.* We set Nicholson down gently and then dressed the entry wound with the second vodka-soaked piece of the shirt.

"You think your Boy Scout first aid is going to help him?" Fowler jeered. "You just wasted perfectly good vodka on him."

He was probably right. What I'd done was Civil War–era medicine.

"Why, hello, offspring," Fowler said, and then started to sing. " 'Welcome, welcome, Christmas Day.' "

I turned and saw him standing a few feet from the twins, holding the shotgun and one of the semiautomatic rifles. His children cowered, crouched against the fireplace.

"Don't be scared, boys and girls," he said. "We're all

in Whoville. And we need everyone to sing and greet Christmas."

"Henry," I said.

He ignored me and shouted, "On your feet! We've got to sing so the Grinch comes down from the mountain!"

Crying, the twins stood up. So did Trey, who turned as pale as a ghost when his father fired the rifle toward the drapes and screamed: "Sing!"

36

THE PHONE RANG AGAIN.

This time Fowler took it. "We're fine!" he yelled and hung up. Then he looked at his children, who'd stopped singing.

"Again!" their father yelled. "Louder! It's got to be heard way up the mountain in the Grinch's cave!"

Fowler was really getting into it now; he'd launched into a second chorus when I stood up and shouted, "Counselor!"

The former civil defense attorney stopped and looked at me dumbly while his children's terrified singing dwindled to sniffling.

"What?" he said. "Don't like Dr. Seuss on Christmas morning, Cross?"

"I love Dr. Seuss on Christmas morning, or on any morning. It's just time for a little cross-examination."

For a moment there was indecision in Fowler's face, then he set the rifle against the fireplace and said, "Sorry, trial's over."

"Call this an appeal, then," I said.

"No appeals!" he shouted, reaching into his pocket and feeding something into his mouth. "There are no appeals in this courtroom."

"But judgments can be overturned," I said, moving toward him.

"There will be no stays of execution."

I looked at him and said softly, "Was it the Huntington's drug case . . . or the vaccine for hepatitis A?"

37

"YOU NEVER TOLD HER?" I ASKED FOWLER. "DIANA DOESN'T KNOW ABOUT those two cases?"

I could see the rage in him building toward release, the rhino about to run. He put the tip of his shotgun right under my chin.

"What don't I know?" Diana cried. "Henry?"

Fowler winced at her voice and then stepped away from me to point the weapon at her. "Shut up, Diana."

"No," she said with withering anger. "I will not shut up. And if my husband is going to die, and my children, I think I deserve to know why."

"It was the lawsuits, Henry," I said. "Wasn't it?"

Fowler said nothing, just stared at his wife as if she were a black hole he would never really fathom.

"What about them?" Diana asked. "Henry? What about the lawsuits?"

Fowler just stood there, a man unhinged, chewing on the source of his own destruction, unable or unwilling to describe its bitterness.

I said, "In one or maybe both of those lawsuits, I believe your husband came into possession of evidence that might have changed the verdicts."

"What?" Diana said, frowning, still looking at her ex-husband. "Is that true? What kind of evidence, Henry?"

He wouldn't look at her.

"Data, medical records, who knows?" I said. "But Henry knew something, and he never revealed the evidence to the people suing the companies he represented. He violated ethics. He broke laws. He destroyed lives. But in the process, he became a very, very wealthy man. And that was good.

"So he tried to compartmentalize, to bury what he'd done, but the problem is that deep down, your ex-husband is a good man, a man of conscience, and it began to eat at him. So he started using liquor and drugs to calm the guilt, and it all went to hell and self-loathing. Is that about right, Henry?"

38

THE ANGER BOILED AGAIN IN FOWLER, SETTING OFF A TWITCH AND A TIC THAT seemed to ripple through his entire body. "You're off by twenty or thirty degrees, Cross."

"Put us straight, then."

He shot Diana a venomous look. "Don't think *you're* not responsible, don't think that you won't be held accountable for what you've done."

"Henry," I said. "Tell us the truth."

Fowler said, "I won the first suit fair and square. But afterward...a year after we won the suit involving the Huntington's drug, I came across data that I'd never seen before, and case files that had never made their way into the proceedings. There was sufficient evidence that the drug accelerated mortality."

"But you never told anyone?"

"And tarnish my stellar reputation?" he asked caustically. "Ruin the family fun? Decrease the speed with which my bitch of a wife was spending the fortune they were paying me? Two million that year. Two million!"

He looked at Diana like he wanted to throttle her. "Every single day I'd come home and hear the gargantuan list of crap she'd bought from this shop or that. Or from a catalog. Or off the Web. Or I'd hear about the cabinet-makers she'd had in. Or the granite-countertop guy. On and on and on!"

Fowler glared at me. "I was trapped."

"But it got worse when you began to represent the hepatitis A vaccine manufacturer?"

He set his jaw and nodded. "That case was almost like you described it, Cross. We were well into trial, and I get this report from an investigator I'd hired to find people who'd taken the hepatitis A vaccine but who weren't part of the class-action suit."

"And?"

"It showed an anomaly among teenagers who'd had the vaccine," he replied. "They seemed to have suffered mild but permanent brain damage because of it."

Diana gasped. "And you didn't tell anybody?"

"*And lose?*" he screamed. "I couldn't lose. You wouldn't let me lose. The kids wouldn't let me. The firm wouldn't let me. And then you start screwing Barry, and the whole thing went to—"

He flipped off the shotgun's safety. "Happy now, Cross? Ready to see the ultimate repercussions of my shredding that private investigator's report?"

39

"WHAT DO YOU THINK KILLING EVERYONE IN THIS ROOM IS GOING TO DO FOR you, Henry?" I asked, glancing at a clock on the mantelpiece and seeing that it was a quarter past seven. "Erase what you've done?"

"Among other things."

I gestured at the phone on the floor. "They've been listening."

He swung the shotgun at me now. "I really don't like you, Cross."

"You can make it right, Henry," I said.

"I'm going to hell for what I've done. I've made my peace with that."

"My grandmother's in her nineties, and she likes to say that every Christmas is a time for rebirth," I said. "I can tell you how you can do that, if you'll let me."

His meth eyes hopped all over me. "You trying to sell me some twelve-step program?"

I made a show of looking at Diana and Dr. Nicholson and the children and then said, "I think you'll want to hear this alone, Henry. You can decide later whether to tell them. We'll go somewhere. The kitchen. Have a cup of coffee. I'll tell you what I think."

"How stupid do you think I am?" Fowler asked. "Yeah, we'll go talk, and then these bastards'll take off."

"Don't be crazy, Henry," Diana said. "I would never leave Barry."

Sadness mixed with loss flickered across his face. Fowler looked at me, reached into his pocket, fed himself something again.

"You taking a visit to the OxyContinent?" I asked.

"So what if I am?"

"Let's go talk," I said, thinking that it was good he was taking a narcotic.

Fowler blinked, then gestured toward the center hall. "My den."

I didn't want Fowler in the den, which was on the opposite side of the house. I wanted him in the kitchen, which was at the rear and overlooked a walled-in garden.

"I could really use some coffee."

The narcotic was hitting Fowler, taking the edge off his high anxiety.

"Sure. We aim to please," he said, then he cracked up and poked me forward with the gun.

We walked to the living room entranceway. Fowler stopped there and spun around. He held his shotgun in the air. For a moment I thought he might fire at the ceiling again. Instead, he spoke to his family with quiet contempt. "I swear to God, if any one of you moves, I will paint the walls with your blood."

40

"WHICH WAY?" I ASKED, KNOWING FULL WELL WHERE THE KITCHEN WAS FROM blueprints Nu had shown me but wanting to seem ignorant and let Fowler think he remained in control.

"Right," he said.

I pivoted and walked down the narrow hallway lined with framed family pictures, my mind whirling with all the ways this move could go bad. What if Diana defied Fowler and tried to get her kids out? What if she tried to run?

We passed the formal dining room on our right. The table was decorated and set like Martha Stewart was coming over for Christmas dinner. I could see the kitchen straight ahead, a light, airy space with lots of windows that looked out at the now leafless ancient oak trees that graced the backyard.

I stepped into the kitchen. Fowler stopped short in the

hallway and said, "I took that photo. I used to call it the most beautiful picture in the world."

I wanted Fowler to come into the kitchen, but he was transfixed and I had to see why. The moment I saw the picture I sensed another dimension to Fowler's madness. One picture, it seemed, was worth a thousand rants.

In the photo, a younger version of Fowler's family sat on the deck of a house that looked to be somewhere on the New England shore, or maybe in Jersey. Five years ago, it must have been, because Trey was a baby in Diana's lap.

Fowler said, "See how perfect they all look, Cross, how... how... blond they are. It's like a catalog... Brooks Brothers... Ralph Lauren. You know where that is? That's Martha's Vineyard, Oak Bluffs. See that house? That house cost me sixty thousand dollars to rent for the month of August. Some people don't make sixty grand in a year. And that's what I was spending on a damn rental in Martha's Vineyard. Those were the days, man. Those were the days, my friend."

41

I FOCUSED ON THE PHOTOGRAPH THAT HENRY FOWLER HAD TAKEN. HIS FAMILY sat smiling naturally in front of a great big weather-beaten house. All three children, even the baby, were wearing charcoal-blue sweaters. And Fowler was right. They looked good. They were tan. Diana's hair was shorter. The kids and the light and Diana really did look beautiful. And everyone looked happy, facing the man who was taking the picture. Henry Fowler. I glanced at him and saw that the pain medicine was swirling in him, putting him in another place and time. I thought about trying to knock the gun from his hands, but he kept it out of reach. I'd pushed him, gotten him to reveal his demons, but I remained unsure if I could get him to give up. I glanced at the clock above the stove. Seven twenty-five a.m. Dr. Nicholson had been shot hours ago. He had to get medical attention. Which meant I needed Fowler in the kitchen. Now.

"God, what a summer," Fowler said in a whisper, still staring at the photo. "We loved it there, all of us. We had an ocean view and a sailboat. Two college kids crewed for us. Every day we ate lobster and fries and clams and blueberry pie. I burned money. Burned money. Thought it would never end."

Tears dripped down his cheeks. "I was the luckiest guy in the whole world, with the best family, the perfect family." His voice turned bitter again and he gripped his gun as if he meant to club someone with it.

I took a step into the kitchen, hoping he'd follow. But Fowler just stood there, looking at the picture. "And then I blew it, Cross. I blew the perfect life."

A small red dot appeared on his left hip, wavered, then began to travel up his body, toward his chest. The sniper Nu and I had ordered into one of the oak trees in the backyard had finally found Fowler through the window.

42

WE'D DECIDED BEFORE I REENTERED THE HOUSE ON THIRTIETH STREET THAT WE couldn't afford to let Dr. Nicholson stay there much past seven thirty. Not if we wanted to have a chance at saving him. If I didn't get Fowler to surrender, it was my job to lure him into the kitchen, where there were windows.

Seeing the red dot on his body, I knew Fowler was dead, and his ex-wife, his children, and Dr. Nicholson had a chance to live.

Fowler saw the dot on his chest and knew it too.

Call it something in my DNA, I don't know. But I couldn't watch this man get shot down on Christmas morning.

I launched myself at him, wrapped him up, gun and all, and drove him hard to the floor.

A rifle shot. Glass broke in a kitchen window. The

picture of Fowler's family shattered as a bullet passed through it and into the wall.

I threw a forearm against the back of Fowler's head, bouncing his face off the hardwood floor, and then ripped the gun from his hands. I got up fast and put my boot on his neck, the muzzle of my gun against his temple. "Henry Fowler, you're under arrest."

By the time I finished reading him his rights, the front door was rammed open, and Nu's men were breaking through the door between the porch and the kitchen. They ran to us, used zip ties on Fowler's ankles and wrists.

Medics rushed into the house. The two SWAT officers lifted Fowler to his feet. He was going to have a hell of a black eye from the pounding he'd taken against the floor.

He stared at me. "Why didn't you let them kill me?"

"Like I said, I believe in the redemptive power of Christmas."

"Not for me." Fowler shook his head. "I'll be in a jail cell. I'll be tortured by what I've done for the rest of my life."

"Unless you testify," I said.

"What?"

"Come forward with what you know. Tell the truth about the Huntington's drug and the hepatitis vaccine. You can still save lives, prevent brain damage."

Fowler stared at me as if this had never occurred to him.

"Merry Christmas, Fowler," I said. Then SWAT took him away.

My eyes began to water, and I wiped them on the back of my sleeve. Maybe what my grandmother had always said about Christmas was true.

"You okay, Alex?" Nu asked.

He'd come in through the broken-down back door.

"Yeah," I said, watching Fowler disappear. "I'm doing fine."

We went to the living room, where McGoey was on top of everything. Crime scene photographers were already snapping away at the broken lamps, the shot-up gifts, and the busted Christmas tree. Social workers were talking to the kids—wiping faces, feeding them fruit, getting them to the bathroom. EMTs were working on Dr. Nicholson.

A gurney was brought through the front door. Two EMT guys slid a board under the badly wounded man. They carefully hoisted him onto the gurney and carried him out.

Diana followed the gurney. She stopped for a second and turned to me.

"God bless you, Detective."

"You too. Take care of your husband, your kids," I told her.

"Somebody close the damn door," Nu shouted. "It's cold in here."

"Yeah, you've got it rough, Adam," I told him.

McGoey smiled and said, "The plan worked. You're a smart guy."

"What if it hadn't worked?" I asked. "What would you be saying then?"

"I'd be saying, 'You're the dumbass who got himself shot on Christmas morning.'"

The three of us took a last look at the living room. I doubted there was much that hadn't been cracked, smashed, broken, or torn.

"God," said McGoey. "Looks like there was one helluva party here."

"Oh, there was," I said. "One helluva party." I shook my head. I felt like I should smile. But I couldn't. I just couldn't.

I looked at my watch. It was nearly eight thirty a.m. I took out my phone and tapped in Bree's name.

"Hey," I said. "Save me some sweet bacon. I'm coming home."

43

SNOW IN WASHINGTON, DC, IS ALWAYS A DISASTER. FOUR INCHES CAN SNARL traffic inside the Beltway. Eight inches will most definitely spawn a nightmare of accidents and near gridlock. True paralysis, however, arrives when the snow depth exceeds fourteen inches, a rare event.

Between ten o'clock on Christmas Eve and ten the following evening, nearly twenty-three inches of snow would blanket the city. It shut down the airport. It shut down the Metro and the bus system. Few cars moved that entire Christmas Day.

At around nine on that Christmas morning, there was only fourteen inches of snow to deal with, but I still couldn't get my car to move. I had to have a Metro patrol unit bring me home. The officer and I had to get out twice to push the stuck cruiser from a drift over on Constitution Avenue. I'd given Nu back his extra boots, and my shoes got soaked and my toes were numb when I reached our home on Fifth Street.

Needless to say, when my family heard the front door open, almost everybody rushed over to kiss me and hug me and wish me merry Christmas. I held Bree tight, said, "This is the best present I could ever get."

But Nana remained seated in her chair, her little throne.

"My, my," she finally said. "Is that my grandson over there? Must be a real special occasion that's got him visiting. Oh, I guess it's Christmas."

I walked to her chair and lifted her up. We stood with our arms around each other, and I never would have imagined a woman that size could have so much strength. She nearly squeezed the air right out of me.

"I just made you some sweet bacon," she said.

"Sweet bacon and a nap sounds just about perfect," I said.

44

EVEN NANA MAMA DECIDED THAT SPENDING CHRISTMAS EVE CONVINCING A crazy man not to kill his family was enough of a reason for me to be excused from attending eleven o'clock mass.

Bree tucked me in and I slept like a dead man for four hours, up until I heard Damon cheering downstairs. He'd become a big hockey fan at prep school and was watching a television broadcast of a game being played at a rink set up inside Fenway Park.

I came downstairs groggily, smelled turkey roasting, and looked at the television. "Snowing in Boston too."

"It's snowing everywhere," Jannie said. "They say it won't stop here until, like, tonight. Kind of a waste, if you ask me."

"Why's that?"

"If it was like two weeks from now, they'd call off school."

"The reporters say you saved a guy's life last night," Damon said.

"Maybe two guys' lives," I replied.

"That's pretty cool."

"A gift, if you think about it."

I spent the rest of the afternoon eating too many cookies, watching the game, holding Bree whenever I could, and listening to my grandmother tell stories about Christmases past while she made yams with little marshmallows, and brussels sprouts with leftover bits of sweet bacon, and a pecan pie that I almost risked my fingers to taste.

"Stay away from that now," Nana kept saying and swatting at my hand.

I taught Damon to carve the turkey when it came out of the oven around five. I carried that platter. Everyone else brought in his or her favorite dish. Damon had the marshmallow yams. Bree had whipped potatoes. Ava brought the cranberry sauce. Jannie carried the stuffing as if she were in a procession.

And, just like every year, someone had to be asked to bring in the brussels sprouts. That would be me.

We sat at the table with cloth napkins, good china, a little crystal for the Christmas wine.

"Alex," Nana said. That was my signal to say grace. We held hands with one another. Bree held mine so tight that I thought she might never let go.

Then I spoke. "Let us thank the Lord for this meal. And also for our health and happiness. And—for being a good family gathered together like this on Christmas Day."

I paused and then said, "Now let us silently give our own personal thanks."

"I'm glad my dad is home!" Damon said and we all smiled.

"Me too," I said.

Then the room went completely silent. The seconds passed. I had a lot to be thankful for: the safety of my family, my own survival, the joy of—

The prayerful silence was broken by Ava.

"I'm hungry. Doesn't the Lord know it's Christmas?"

We all laughed. And then the bowls and platters of food were passed around. And just as we started to dig in, my cell phone rang.

CHAPTER

45

BEFORE THE PHONE JANGLED, EVERYONE HAD BEEN HAPPY, THRILLED TO HAVE
me home at last, safe and sound. Now every face fell.

Nana shook a butter knife at me. "Don't you dare answer that, Alex. Don't you dare."

Though everyone had been fine once I got home, I knew the hostage situation had taken its toll. Not only had I been in danger, but I had missed our family traditions. I had not been home to sing carols and put the kids to bed on Christmas Eve. I had not been up at dawn with Nana Mama to stuff the stockings. I had not been there to watch my children open their presents, and I had not been around to help make sweet bacon.

I glanced at the caller ID, smiled, and said, "It's Ali."

My six-year-old son was with his mother, Christine, for the holiday. Everyone's shoulders relaxed. Bree grinned, got up, and said, "I'll warm that pie."

"Merry Christmas," I said as I picked up the phone.

"God bless us, every one!" Ali cried.

"Watching *Scrooge*?" I asked.

"Last night," Ali said. "Thank you for the boxing gloves."

"You're welcome."

"Mommy doesn't like them."

"You just bring them home with you, then."

"Santa gave me an Xbox. What did he get you?"

"Seventeen inches of snow, and the best little boy in the world," I replied.

He laughed and boasted, "I went sledding in the park."

"Fun?"

"We built a jump."

"Then it had to be fun," I said. "Do you want to say hello to Nana and everyone?"

He said he did and I passed the phone down the table to my grandmother, watching her light up as she listened. "Well, God bless us, every one, to you too, little man," she said.

I felt a hand on my shoulder and looked up to see Bree back from the kitchen, silhouetted against the fading day. My wife smiled and kissed me on the cheek. She smelled wonderful when she leaned over and whispered, "You'll be getting a special gift later."

I smiled and squeezed her hand, feeling that, for at least a little while, nothing could possibly wreck our well-deserved celebration.

46

AT 5:19 THAT CHRISTMAS AFTERNOON, A WOMAN CARRYING A U.S. PASSPORT that identified her as Julia Azizz of Philadelphia tipped the Diamond Cab driver extremely well for bringing her all the way from Arlington, Virginia, to DC in the horrible weather. Then she got out of the taxi at the Massachusetts Avenue entrance to Union Station, north of Capitol Hill.

Azizz shivered in the frigid wind and stepped into deep snow that workers were struggling to clear. The light was fading, but for the moment she kept her sunglasses on as she lugged a large, heavy shopping bag from Macy's toward the station door.

A small, fit, and exotically attractive woman with burnished copper skin, Azizz wore a dark wool coat, gray cashmere scarf, dark wool slacks, and a ribbed turtleneck sweater. A pair of calf-high black leather boots completed the look, an outfit that suggested she was perhaps some stylish congressional aide instead of a fanatical member of Al Ayla, the Family.

Azizz's real first name was Hala.

A plague upon them, she thought as she pushed her way through the revolving doors into the vaulted marble Amtrak facility. Hala was pleased to see that what she'd heard on the taxi radio on the way into the city was true: though everything else had come to a near stand-still, Amtrak trains were still running. They were heavily delayed by the storm, though, and Union Station was packed with travelers.

It was perfect. Even better than she'd planned.

Indeed, the events that were about to unfold were supposed to have taken place earlier in the day, around eleven, give or take ten minutes. But the storm had changed things, delayed the intricate timing of her plot by some five hours at least, the last time she'd checked.

Kicking the snow off her boots, she looked around the main hall, ignoring the voice of Nat King Cole crooning about chestnuts on an open fire, paying no attention to the Christmas trees and lights, the token menorah, and the darkened shops to her left and right. She saw only the long lines at the ticket counters ahead of her and the scores of anxious travelers sitting on benches and on the floor, some groggy from Christmas dinner and eager to be on their way home, others frus-trated and hungry because they still hadn't gotten to their holiday feasts, having been separated from their families by the freak storm.

Hala felt no pity whatsoever for any of them. As far as she was concerned, they were pigs who ignored the teachings of their own prophet Isa, swine who believed in only what they could buy, drink, or stuff down their fat throats.

Americans are weak. They know nothing of sacrifice, or of God.

She flipped open a throwaway cell phone and hit Redial.

"Yes?" a male voice answered in Arabic.

"Why?" Hala asked.

"One, four, and zero," he replied.

She glanced at the big clock inside the station. It was 5:25. She calculated and then said, "Seven and five."

"Inshallah," the man replied and hung up.

Hala stuffed the phone in her pocket, thinking, *And now, finally, it begins.*

She almost smiled at that thought before reaching up to remove her sunglasses and scarf. She'd grown her hair out recently and stopped dying it auburn. Now luxuriously thick, long, and near jet-black, her hair was pulled back severely into a bun so that her face, with its extraordinary bone structure, was visible to everyone, infidel and believer alike.

Indeed, that's how Hala wanted it. She looked around at a young family moving toward the ticket line.

She flashed on her own children, Fahd and Aamina, back in Saudi Arabia, abandoned to her mother while Hala fought and sacrificed for God. Seeing her young son and daughter in her mind now, seeing them that last time in her husband's arms, Hala felt a moment of desperate, almost crippling grief, but she quickly compartmentalized the emotion, used her husband's death and the soon-to-be-eternal rift between her and her children to fuel her anger, and her will.

Her head felt light, speedy, undulating. Stuffing the scarf and sunglasses into the Macy's bag, Hala understood that this was what it was like to be a martyr, to give one's soul over to the Eternal One.

She was at peace with it, submissive even.

Hala looked around, spotted security cameras aimed at various angles inside the station. Before going in search of something to eat, she made a point of walking in front of each and every one of those cameras, looking right up into the lens and giving the people watching a nice icy smile.

CHAPTER

47

SHORTLY AFTER THE PECAN PIE WITH VANILLA ICE CREAM WAS DEMOLISHED AND the dishes cleared, Nana Mama began to read out loud from the King James Bible and the Gospel of Saint Luke: "'And it came to pass in those days, that there went out a decree from Caesar Augustus, that all the world should be taxed. And all went to be taxed, every one into his own city. And Joseph also went up from Galilee, out of the city of Nazareth, into Judaea, to the city of David, which is called Bethlehem, to be taxed with Mary his espoused wife, being great with child.'"

My grandmother has been reading Luke's account of Jesus's birth after every Christmas dinner since I came to live with her, when I was ten. As exhausted as I was, hearing her recount the circumstances of Jesus's birth, I felt rooted by the words of the Bible and connected by the strength of Nana Mama's moving delivery. Bree was sitting in my lap, and I hugged her and laid my head against her back, listening to her heartbeat and feeling like I could drift off to sleep a very happy man.

But then my cell phone rang again.

Nana Mama stopped reading and shot me a withering look. I glanced at the caller ID. There was no name, but I knew that number, or a variation of it. The call was coming from someone inside the Federal Bureau of Investigation, where I used to work as a criminal profiler.

I winced at the reaction I knew I was going to get, but I whispered, "I *have* to take this. Keep going."

Stonily, Bree stood to let me up. Stonily, Nana Mama read on, raising her voice as I left the room, calling after me as I headed into the kitchen: "'And she brought forth her firstborn son, and wrapped him in swaddling clothes, and laid him in a manger; because there was no room for them in the inn.'"

"Alex Cross," I said, kneading at the pain growing between my eyes.

"How fast can you get to Louisiana and D Street?" asked Ned Mahoney, an old friend and special agent I used to work cases with at the Bureau.

"Tomorrow," I said, suppressing a yawn. "Maybe the day after."

"I'm sending a car for you."

"It's Christmas."

"I know it's Christmas," Mahoney snapped. "That's why I need *you.*"

"Ned, I've got a very angry ninety-something-year-old

grandmother shouting the Gospel of Saint Luke at me, and—"

"We think it's Hala Al Dossari, Alex," Mahoney said.

A chill spiked through me, got me wide awake. "You think Dr. Al Dossari's at Louisiana and D?"

"Worse," Mahoney said. "Inside Union Station. And she's carrying a very big Macy's shopping bag."

"Shit," I said.

"Uh-huh," Mahoney said. "I'm sending a four-wheel-drive vehicle to you. I expect you to get in it."

He hung up as if there were no counterargument to be made.

Out in the dining room, my grandmother was still reading, even louder than before. "'And the angel said to them, Fear not: for, behold—'"

I returned to the dining room and Nana Mama stopped, studied me for a long moment, read it all in my body language. "Are you needed again, Alex?"

I saw faces clouding, my wife's included.

"It's a sad fact of life that not everyone believes in peace on earth and goodwill toward men," I said. "The FBI's sending a vehicle to pick me up."

48

AS DARKNESS TOOK CHRISTMAS DAY, THERE WERE ONLY FIVE FOOD PLACES open inside Union Station: Pizzeria Uno on the mezzanine level; McDonald's and Sbarro, in the northeast and northwest corners of the station; and Great Wraps and Nothing But Doughnuts on the lower level, northwest side.

Hala bought a gyro at the Great Wraps and devoured it, thinking that this might well be her last meal. She was fine with that. Though the sandwich was mediocre at best, the spiced meat made her think of home and of Tariq barbecuing a lamb behind their house as part of the celebration for her daughter's first birthday. It had been one of the best days of her life, and she clung to that memory as she waited for the group of Japanese tourists at the next table to get up and head to the escalator back to street level. Hala slipped in among them, carrying the

Macy's bag low enough that, she hoped, the security camera would be blocked from seeing it.

Upstairs, she plotted her way across the rear of the station, choreographing every step so the cameras would get only glimpses of her.

It was 5:47, twenty-two minutes since she'd shown her face to the cameras. She figured there was zero chance that the police had been alerted to her presence yet. That meant at least twenty-five minutes before there could be any direct response. She added ten, maybe fifteen minutes because of the snow, and decided that she'd see the first indication of law enforcement somewhere around 6:25.

Hala headed east through the station, passing the dark entrance to the MARC suburban rail lines on her left and the staircase down to Amtrak gates A through L. With the rear of the ticket counter to her right, she glanced overhead at the board giving approximate times of train arrivals and departures.

The Northeast Corridor Acela Express 2166 was leaving for New York City and Boston in fifteen minutes, approximately four hours late. The next Acela was due to leave at 6:50, also several hours late. But the Crescent, heading south to Atlanta and New Orleans, was only thirty minutes behind, scheduled to depart at 7:30.

Perfect.

Hala pushed on, weaving in and out of the crowd, doing her best to keep other people close to her as she headed to the McDonald's, which was jammed. She slid into the crowded restaurant, skirting those waiting to order, and grabbed a small soda cup someone had left on an empty table.

She transferred the cup to her left hand, paused a moment, and then brought her right index finger to her lips, moistened it with her tongue, and reached into her coat pocket. Her finger found a clear pharmaceutical capsule that stuck to her saliva. She waited until the soda counter cleared, then angled quickly at it.

Hala moved the cup to her right hand, the capsule still stuck to her finger. She held the cup up to the Coke nozzle, pressed on the lever, and filled the cup halfway. Pleased to sense no one in line behind her, she acted as if she were waiting for the fizz to settle and moved the cup slightly left, giving her right finger access to the bottom of the nozzle.

Hala crammed the capsule up into the dripping nozzle, felt it lodge, and quickly moved her hand away. She pressed the water lever, rinsed her finger in case the enzymes in her saliva had made the capsule leak, and headed toward the customers waiting to order, not once looking back.

She stood there at the end of the line closest to the exit into the rail station, imagining the poison melting up in the nozzle, imagining someone getting a Coke, trying to decide how long it might take until some people started dying and others started screaming.

49

HALA AL DOSSARI IS BACK IN DC, I THOUGHT, SITTING IN THE PASSENGER seat of a blue Jeep Grand Cherokee that had come to get me.

A doctor by training, a jihadist by choice, Hala was a member of Al Ayla, the Family, a terrorist organization seeded and rooted in the kingdom of Saudi Arabia and subsequently transplanted to the United States. At the moment, Hala occupied slot number six on the FBI's ten most wanted list, sought in connection with the poisoning of the Washington, DC, water supply the prior summer and suspected in the murders of at least six Saudi expatriates, including her late husband, Tariq.

I understood why Mahoney had called me. We'd worked together trying to catch Al Dossari after the water incident. I'd even helped construct an extensive profile of her.

But my mind would not call up the details. As we drove through the city, I stared out the windows. I couldn't believe how much snow there was. It looked like an avalanche had hit Washington. But wreaths still hung on doors, and Christmas trees still lit windows. Seemed like everybody in the District had given up on going outside and settled in for a sweet night. Everybody, of course, except me.

When do I start saying no, I thought, *instead of just reacting to whatever crisis life sends my way? When do I begin to live Alex Cross's life? I mean* really *live it.* Here I was, blessed with terrific kids and a grandmother who was as healthy as a twenty-year-old and as smart as the Sphinx. And then there was the miracle of Bree. I'd found someone wonderful to love me just when I'd thought romance had left me lame at the starting gate.

When was I going to have the chance to enjoy life?

I called home, wanting at least to tell Bree that I was feeling these things.

The phone at my house rang. Then it rang some more. And some more. Then the damn thing kept ringing. In my mind, I could see and hear the scene at home where that phone was ringing.

Nana Mama would most likely say something like "If you don't want a slap on the wrist, then I advise you not to answer the phone."

"But Nana," Damon would say, "what if it isn't Dad calling? What if it's somebody else?"

"Well, whoever it is should have called earlier," she would reply.

"What if it's an emergency?"

"They should call 911."

I hung up and then pressed Redial. The ringing started in again, and I had a vision of Nana coolly saying something along the lines of "I wonder who that could be?"

I hung up and stared morosely out the window. My family knew what a detective's life was like. Bad guys don't take holidays. They show up anytime, anyplace. Not just on a summer Sunday afternoon when you're sitting and painting a fence, but also on a Christmas afternoon when you're sitting and having dinner.

They all knew my job was an emergency-type job, like being a doctor or a firefighter. On top of that, it was a tough job. And beyond that...beyond that...Well, beyond that, I wished someone would answer the damn phone. Because they were my family, and I was really missing them.

That longing remained as we passed through police lines that closed off Louisiana Avenue for two blocks between C Street and Massachusetts Avenue, including most of lower Senate Park. The road had already been plowed on both sides. But the only vehicles visible on that stretch of Louisiana were two black motor homes idling near D Street, wheels buried in the snow.

CHAPTER

50

I RECOGNIZED THE VEHICLES IN AN INSTANT. BOTH WERE FBI MOBILE command centers, probably brought over from the parking garage beneath the J. Edgar Hoover Building on Pennsylvania Avenue. The Jeep stopped beside the forward command center and I climbed out.

The wind was picking up, penetrating the blue police parka and Washington Redskins wool hat I wore, and I hustled to the door of the mobile command center. I happened to glance beneath it and saw barely any snow there at all. The door opened with a whoosh, distracting me. I climbed up the stairs and found Ned Mahoney waiting.

Lean, intense, with distinctive gray-blue eyes, Mahoney had once run the FBI's Hostage Rescue Team, which also served as the Bureau's domestic counterterrorism unit. Until recently, Mahoney had been in charge of specialized training for agents up and down the East Coast; now he ran a new rapid-response operation that the Bureau activated in times of crisis, like this one. Beyond him stood Bobby Sparks, taller than Mahoney, early thirties, and currently the East Coast HRT leader. Both men were dressed casually.

I shook hands with them, said, "You know for sure she's in there?"

"If it's not her, it's her twin," Mahoney said. "She paraded through the main hall, gave the cameras a show. Since then she's shown a fairly sophisticated understanding of the cameras, their positions, and their limitations. She's in the food court downstairs."

He gestured over his shoulder at three FBI agents working a bank of screens. "We're tied into every camera in the station, and the memory banks."

I followed him and stood behind the agents, looking at screens that showed various scenes inside the train station, including one in the lower food court. "Where is she?"

An agent, a woman with close-cropped reddish hair, tapped the food-court feed, said, "She went there, to the right side of the escalator, just outside of range. There's no way out of there, and she's in plain sight of everyone else."

"How long's she been there?"

"Five minutes, tops," Bobby Sparks said. "Twenty-three inside total."

"And you guys are already here?" I asked.

Mahoney did not answer for a moment. Bobby Sparks said, "We're quick."

I squinted, realizing what I'd seen outside. "No, you're not. There's no snow under this bus, which means it was parked here before the storm started."

The FBI agent looked annoyed. "Nothing gets by you, does it?"

"Rarely," I said. "Level with me, gentlemen."

Sparks appeared conflicted, but Mahoney said to one of the agents working at the screens, "Call up the Mokiri interrogation. Fast."

51

THE AGENT TYPED SEVERAL COMMANDS, AND GRAINY FOOTAGE APPEARED: A swarthy man in his late thirties strapped to a chair and glaring defiantly at a man in a denim outfit who had his back to us.

"Guy in the chair is Abdul Mokiri. He's Syrian, here on a research grant at Tulane University. He's also a member of Al Ayla, and he trained with Hala Al Dossari and her husband in Saudi Arabia three years ago."

"Where's she gone? What is she doing?" the man with his back to the camera demanded. "Hala?"

"You can't do this," Mokiri said. "I have the civil rights."

"You only have rights if you're in America," the man we couldn't see said. "And let me assure you, you're not in America, Abdul, and therefore we do not play by American rules."

The Syrian spit at the interrogator. Someone very big, his upper body and face lost in the shadows, pushed Mokiri's chair forward and up close to a card table that had been blocked from view by the interrogator. The same person grabbed the terrorist's right hand and stretched it toward something on the table I did not recognize at first. Mokiri began to squirm, and he shouted, "You can't do this!"

The hot plate turned brilliant red. Mokiri's hand was lowered toward the coils.

"Shut it off," I said.

The agent did. I glared at Mahoney and Bobby Sparks as intensely as the Syrian had at his interrogator. "Didn't know the Bureau participated in torture, Ned."

"It doesn't," Mahoney shot back. "I don't know where it came from, Alex. I don't want to know where it came from. But I'm glad I know what Mokiri spilled."

"Confessions made under torture can't be taken seriously," I said. "They're half-truths mixed with what the tortured person thinks the torturer wants to hear."

"Maybe," Bobby Sparks said stonily. "But we didn't have the luxury of thinking that way when Mokiri said that Hala was planning to bomb Union Station on Christmas morning."

"She's kind of late," I said.

"Snowstorm," Mahoney said.

I closed my eyes. "But she's in there now? No doubt?"

"Show him those videos of her coming into the station," Mahoney told another one of the agents working the screens.

A moment later, several of the lower feeds showed Hala Al Dossari moving about the south side of the main hall looking directly at the cameras.

"She had to have known we run facial-recognition software on everyone who enters that station," I said.

"It's been written about," Mahoney agreed. "And she certainly seemed to want us to see her in there."

"Right, but why?"

"We were hoping you might have some insight on that."

I shrugged, trying to get my brain to think clearly. "She could be trying to lure you guys in there so she can detonate and kill a bunch of federal agents."

"That occurred to us," Bobby Sparks said.

"Okay. Any other information I need to know?"

Mahoney nodded. "We've had NSA targeting the station since yesterday afternoon, picking up all mobile transmissions. Only one seems pertinent."

The agent with the red hair gave her computer an order. The interior of the command center filled with whispers in what I guessed was Arabic, a woman speaking with a man.

Bobby Sparks said, "That's her twenty-five minutes ago, after she entered the station. She says, 'Why?' Then the unidentified male replies, 'One, four, and zero.' She says, 'Seven and five.' Unidentified male replies, 'Inshallah.'"

"So a code?" I asked.

"Obviously," Mahoney said.

"Give me a break, Ned," I said. "I'm running on fumes here. You get a location on the guy's cell?"

"We pinged the towers," Mahoney replied. "He was in the Suitland–Silver Hill area, but we didn't have enough time to get him located better."

Before I could filter that, the third agent working the camera surveillance inside Union Station tapped his headset and said, "Sorry to interrupt, but we've got someone down and dead inside the McDonald's, street level, northeast corner of the station."

52

SIX MINUTES BEFORE, AS WHITE FOAM CAME FROM THE MOUTH OF A convulsing pimply-faced homeboy in his late teens and people began to shout for help, Hala had slipped from the McDonald's and taken four big, easy steps diagonally with her back to the nearest security camera. She was inside the women's restroom in fewer than six seconds.

She walked the length of the stalls until she spotted one with a metal grate in the wall above it. Luckily, the stall was open. She entered, still hearing shouts of alarm outside the restroom, turned, and went to work, knowing full well that the poisoning would quickly bring DC police to the area, police who would soon figure out that a suspect matching her description had been at the fountain a few minutes before the homeboy got his Coke. And so the police would join the others, probably FBI, already looking for her.

Six minutes. That's all she gave herself.

Hala opened the Macy's bag and retrieved a blue workman's suit that had a patch sewn to the chest that said AMTRAK and beneath it the name SEAN. She tore off her jacket, removed her boots, and climbed into the jumpsuit. Around her neck, she hung a chain attached to a remarkably good forgery of an Amtrak employee card that identified her as Sean Belmont, a member of an emergency-train-repair crew.

Four minutes left. She scrubbed her face, lashes, and brows free of all makeup. She slid on workman's boots and then tucked her hair up under a wig that featured short blond hair in a masculine cut. She put in contact lenses that turned her eyes blue and painted her face and hands with pale makeup.

Ninety seconds to go. Hala stood up on the toilet, which put the metal grate at about shoulder height. She could look through it into a length of air duct about eighteen inches wide and thirteen high. She glanced at the stalls on either side of her and was heartened to see them empty. Quick as she dared, she tried the screws holding the grate over the duct and found them loose. She had the grate off and balanced on the toilet in less than thirty seconds.

Hala reached inside and groped until she found the sound-suppressed pistol taped there. She tore it off, duct tape and all, stepped off the toilet, and dropped the gun into the battered canvas tool kit in the Macy's bag. She retrieved the tool kit and set it aside. Then she reached to the bottom of the bag and took out eight Christmas-paper-wrapped boxes, each about the size of a large coffee cup. She put them in the tool kit. The jacket and high-heeled boots went in the Macy's bag.

Forty seconds.

Hala got back on the toilet with the Macy's bag. She shoved the bag into the duct hard, sending it in deep, and then refitted the grate.

Ten seconds. The restroom door opened. A girl squealed, "OMG! Did you see the stuff coming out his mouth?"

"I'm gonna be sick, you keep talking about it," another girl replied.

Hala grabbed the tool bag, opened the stall, and went right at them. "Sorry, young ladies," she said in the deepest voice she could muster. "We had a leak back there. She's all yours now."

"You coulda, like, put up a sign or something," the OMG girl said indignantly.

"Too much snow," Hala said, as if there were some connection, and exited the restroom.

She made a sharp right, ignoring the commotion unfolding in and outside of the McDonald's to her immediate left. She walked resolutely west toward the entrance to the Amtrak gates and glanced to her left only once, when she picked up in her peripheral vision a big guy wearing a blue MPD parka and two shorter men wearing vests that said FBI. A sweaty man in an Amtrak police uniform followed the three of them into the McDonald's.

Hala allowed herself the barest grin. That had flushed them out, hadn't it?

She had no idea who the FBI agents were and guessed the sweaty guy was the Amtrak officer in charge tonight. But she totally recognized Alex Cross, the guy who found the president's kidnapped kids. He'd been all over the papers.

In an odd way, Hala felt honored.

53

I KNELT OVER THE BODY OF PHILLIP LAMONTE, WHO DRESSED THE GANGSTA BUT whose identification showed he was a junior at Catholic University. He had a home address on Manhattan's Upper West Side and carried a ticket to Penn Station on the Acela that was about to board. The extra-large cup lay on the floor next to him. The ice in it hadn't yet melted.

I lowered my face over the foam around his mouth and sniffed. I smelled an acrid odor I recognized.

"Cyanide poisoning," I said.

"Hala?" Mahoney said.

"Has to be," I replied. "That's how she killed her husband, right?"

"That's how he died," Bobby Sparks agreed.

I looked at the closest patrol officer. "Was this guy with anyone?"

The cop gestured with her chin toward a skinny white

kid, late teens, who was also dressed to party with 50 Cent and Diddy. "Name's Allen Kent."

I glanced at the cup. "Phillip drinking from that before he died?" I asked Kent.

The kid nodded, but he was obviously in shock.

"Anyone else get close to that drink, son?" I asked.

Kent shook his head. "Phil got it himself from the fountain."

I didn't know how she'd done it, but I was certain Hala Al Dossari had murdered this college kid. And how didn't seem to matter as much as why.

I looked at Mahoney and Sparks, said, "Close this place down."

Captain Seymour Johnson, the shift commander of the Amtrak police, a sweaty, unhealthy-looking man, lost more color. "Are you crazy? We're the only transportation into or out of DC. We don't even know if this woman is still in here, for God's sake."

"Maybe she's not," I said. "But if I were you, I'd put men with her picture at every exit. No one gets out of Union Station without proper identification. That goes for passengers who are boarding too. And call in Metro homicide and patrol. There's deep snow everywhere. If she has made it outside and doesn't have a car, then she's on foot and visible."

Mahoney agreed and started making calls. Bobby Sparks did the same. So did Johnson. I looked around, spotted a guy, early thirties, wearing a chesterfield over-coat, watching. He held an iPad.

I went to him. "You see what happened, Mr. . . . . ?"

"Goldberg. Jared Goldberg. And no, I didn't see any-thing. I came over when I heard the screaming."

"You a patriot, Mr. Goldberg?" I asked.

His brows knit. "I like to think so."

I handed him my card, said, "Alex Cross. I work with Metro DC Police and as a consultant to the FBI. Can you help me?"

Goldberg frowned. "I clerk at the tax court. How can I—"

"Your iPad," I said. "Work on one of those 4G net-works?"

He nodded.

"Backed up in—what do they call it—the iCloud or something?"

The law clerk frowned but nodded again.

"Good, can I use it?" I asked. "I promise you I'll return it. And if I break it, I'll replace it with one even better."

Goldberg looked pained, but he handed it over.

"What are you up to, Cross?" asked Bobby Sparks when he saw me return with the iPad in hand.

"Those guys out in the command center," I said. "Can they transmit the footage from the cameras at this end of the station?"

The HRT commander thought, then said, "They'll have to feed it through one of our secure websites, but affir-mative, I think they can do that."

54

AT THE OPPOSITE END OF THE RAIL STATION, INSIDE THE MEN'S ROOM NOW, Hala had again taken a stall that featured a duct grate above it. She waited until the stalls adjacent to hers emptied, and then, for the second time in the past few minutes, removed already loosened screws. She turned the grate sideways and pushed it deep into the duct.

She had to stand there for several minutes while an old man came in and urinated, but then he left and the place fell silent.

Slight in stature, Hala had been a highly competitive gymnast as a girl and still maintained her agility and limberness. After shoving the tool kit in after the grate, she stood up on the exposed pipe of the toilet, grasped the stall walls on either side of her, tightened her abdomen, and swung her legs up into a pike position, toes pointed almost at the ceiling.

The split second she felt her hips about to fall, she snapped her heels and calves forward into the open duct. Wriggling, she was completely inside the ventilation system within ten seconds. She kept wriggling and scooting, pushing the tool bag and the grate ahead of her, deeper into the duct.

Three feet in was an intersection of four ducts. She turned her upper body into the right-side passage, pulled herself totally in, and then inched back across the one she'd just left. It took some straining with her left hand, but she was able to retrieve the grate.

Looking toward the light shining in through the open hole in the wall to the restroom, she crabbed back to it and then peered out. A boy was peeing with his father. Hala looked at them from the darkness of the ductwork, wondering if this was something Tariq had ever done with their son, Fahd. Had her boy ever been that young?

When they left, Hala shook off whatever regrets she had and pulled the grate back over the open duct, securing it with an eight-inch length of picture-frame wire she'd brought along for that purpose. Two minutes later, she'd gotten herself turned around again, and she pushed on, straight down the main duct, smelling the odor of pizzas cooking at Sbarro pouring into the air-vent system from her left.

She felt her stomach grumble, ignored it, and kept wriggling. Twenty-five feet farther on, Hala reached a second intersection in the ductwork; she arched and pulled her way into the one that broke right, heading north. When she was fully inside that duct, she stopped, chest heaving, got out the disposable cell from the pocket of the workman's suit, and hit Redial.

"Why?" she whispered.

"Four and zero," the male voice replied.

Her allies were close to the target now—it would have taken them no more than twelve minutes to get there on an ordinary day, but the snow had changed everything. Still, she trusted his judgment.

"Go with God," she said, and hung up.

After stowing the cell phone, she slid on another ten feet, to where the duct made a ninety-degree left turn. In the north wall there was another grate. Cold air was blowing through it. Hala shivered; she paused for only a second to look through the grate, finding herself high above dimly lit loading platforms and two commuter trains sitting dark on the suburban rail tracks.

Hala crawled on toward a third grate. She moved stealthily, as if she were sliding into position for a sniper's shot, which she was. The last ten feet took nearly ten minutes, leaving her twenty-eight minutes before her role turned crucial.

Irritating Christmas music blared from somewhere. Hala peered through the grate. She was fifteen feet up the east wall of a loading dock platform owned by the U.S. Postal Service. Directly below her were large canvas hampers holding canvas bags that were filled with mail. A skeleton crew of three men worked on the dock, transferring the mailbags from the hampers into an open compartment at the rear of a railcar.

Hala flashed on an image of herself much younger, out

in the desert with Tariq, before the children came. He was teaching her how to shoot a pistol. How odd it had been, that aiming and firing a gun came so naturally to her. Then again, shooting was something precise, like medicine, where attention to technique and detail came together to create a little miracle. And wasn't that what a perfectly placed shot was? A little miracle? A gift from God?

Hala thought so. She got the silenced Glock out of the tool bag and aimed down through the slats of the grate at a fat Latino guy with muttonchops. He was farthest from her, closest to the tracks. The one most likely to get away.

55

BOBBY SPARKS AND MAHONEY COMMANDEERED OTHER IPADS WITHIN MINUTES of seeing what I was up to. With the tablets we could be two, three, or four places at once. The rail station itself had become our movable crisis center. We could manipulate time as well—backward, anyway.

I had all the feeds from the three cameras in and around the northeast end of the station, the ones closest to the McDonald's, run back to the approximate time of Phillip LaMonte's collapse. I heard the shouts and saw Hala Al Dossari slipping out in the commotion and disappearing in the direction of the ladies' room to the left of the restaurant. None of the cameras faced the restroom directly, but it was clear that that's where she was going.

"Block it off," Bobby Sparks barked at Johnson, the Amtrak police commander. Then the FBI hostage rescue leader led the way in, badge up, gun out, with Mahoney and me bringing up the rear.

We found three women inside. One was in her eighties, an older lady who put me in mind of Nana, and a younger, prettier woman who nonetheless didn't hold a candle to Bree. The third was a girl in her late teens, plump where Hala Al Dossari was thin.

When they'd left, we searched the restroom from top to bottom. The toilet stalls had not been serviced since before the storm. Wearing latex gloves, I got down on my hands and knees and peered into each one. I spotted an off-white blotch on the floor of the third.

I got out a pencil and poked at it with the eraser, saw it smear.

"What do you have, Alex?" Mahoney asked.

"Looks like makeup," I said.

"In a ladies' room," Bobby Sparks said. "Imagine that."

I got back to my feet and noticed the grate above the toilet. I didn't see how anyone could've gotten into such a small space, but then again, I'm six two and more than two hundred pounds.

I slid a fingernail into one of the screws and was interested to find it loose. "Got a flashlight?" I asked.

Mahoney produced a mini Maglite. I flipped it on, shone it through the slats, and saw about six feet away the crumpled Macy's bag Hala Al Dossari had been carrying.

CHAPTER

56

I DRAGGED THE BAG OUT WITH A MOP HANDLE MAHONEY FOUND.

"Her boots and the jacket," I said. "Nothing in the pockets."

"I'll take that," Mahoney said. "I want it checked for explosive residue."

"We need the feeds of all cameras in the station in the ten minutes or so after LaMonte died," I said, heading out of the restroom.

Two minutes later, an FBI technician was running a swab test on the Macy's bag, and I was looking at a long-angle shot of the northeast end of Union Station, the feed from the only camera that gave us a reasonable view of the area around the restroom. I sped it up, checking out everyone walking west of the McDonald's.

"There we are," Mahoney said, pointing to the image of the four of us hurrying toward the McDonald's.

But I was staring at the man who'd glanced at us as we'd passed, a slight figure with sandy-colored hair who was wearing a workman's jumpsuit that said AMTRAK and carrying a canvas tool bag.

"That's off," I said.

"What?" Mahoney asked.

"That tool bag," I said. "It's the kind of thing plumbers used to carry. Or masons. I don't see a modern workman with something like that."

The figure disappeared from view.

"Where's he going?" Mahoney asked.

We were standing back out in the main hall by then. I looked around, orienting myself to the camera's angle, and let my eye travel in the direction the workman had taken, seeing the tail end of a line of people clearing security and climbing down the stairs to Amtrak gates A through L.

"There's an Acela leaving soon," I said, running toward the line while Mahoney called out to the command center out on Louisiana Avenue, asking for all footage of the security gate since it had opened for boarding.

We had it in less than thirty seconds. I replayed it at four times the normal speed and quickly spotted the workman with the canvas bag. But he wasn't in line for the Acela. He skirted the gate and walked all the way to the other end of the station, where he entered the men's restroom.

We began to run. My phone rang. Bree.

"Alex?"

"I can't talk," I said. "I want to talk. More than you know, but I can't."

"What's going on?"

"All I can say is that there is a very, very bad person in Union Station."

"Give me a great Christmas present. Stay away from him."

"It's a woman, and I promise you I'll try."

57

HALA TOOK A SLOW, DEEP BREATH, DROPPED THE TENSION FROM HER shoulders, and dwelled within the sight picture she had over the barrel of the suppressed pistol. The big Hispanic postal worker with the muttonchops turned from the open railcar and took two steps before she squeezed the trigger.

The pop the suppressed gun made going off seemed loud to her in the duct. But neither of the other two postal workers reacted until Muttonchops fell to his knees, hands trying to stop the blood from gushing out of the hole she'd put through his windpipe.

The second postal worker was bald. His pale skull made an easy target for her next shot, which went through the back of his head. The third worker, a thin black guy, seemed to have figured out he was next, because he ducked and ran zigzags across the loading dock, screaming for help.

He didn't get any. Hala's third shot shattered his pelvis as he tried to climb the stairs leading to the main postal facility. His legs buckled, leaving him howling at the bottom of the steps. Her fourth shot hit him in the chest, and he sagged forward.

Hala returned the gun to the tool bag and got out a power screwdriver fitted with a tungsten-coated drill bit. In less than two minutes, she'd reamed out the mounts holding the four screws and gripped the grate by the slats.

She felt the grate come free of the wall, moved it out, and then flicked it hard to her right. It clanged to the floor. After grabbing the tool bag, she wriggled her arms and shoulders free of the duct, looked right below her, and realized she wouldn't need the thin rope she'd brought along.

Hala tossed the tool bag to her left, saw it land in one of the mail hampers. She focused on the hamper fifteen feet directly below her and squirmed free of the hole up to the top of her hips, then rotated so her back faced the wall. She let herself hang down it, felt her hips and legs begin to slide free of the duct.

The instant Hala felt the edge scrape the backs of her calves, she arched her spine, pushed her belly forward, and then let all that tension go in a snapping action. Her legs flipped her out and over the duct. As she fell, she rotated her legs around, as if she were dismounting off the balance beams of her childhood; her head glanced off the wall before she landed in a jolting squat that pulled something sharply in her left hip.

Hala grunted, fought the pain, rolled over the metal rim of the hamper's frame, and got to the floor. A moment later, she had the tool bag. She winced as she went by the dead postal workers, trying to compensate for a torn muscle; the psoas or the iliacus, by the feel of it.

This would not do. She stopped, set the bag down by Muttonchops, dug in her pocket for a baggie with pills she'd stuffed there. She found one ten-milligram OxyContin tablet and an eight-hundred-milligram ibuprofen. One for pain. One for swelling.

The fiery sensation spreading through her hip had not lessened by the time she reached the edge of the loading dock. She flinched as she got down and then crawled backward off the edge of the dock, the cold night breeze on her cheeks, knowing how much it was going to hurt to drop just three feet.

What I feel doesn't matter, she thought as she pushed off.

But when she landed beside the postal railcar, she felt the pain like a knife shoved into her. Hala gasped and stumbled, dropped the canvas bag, squeezed her eyes shut, and bit her lip to keep from screaming.

CHAPTER

58

WE RAN TO THE MEN'S RESTROOM WHERE I WAS SURE HALA HAD GONE IN disguise. Halfway there, Mahoney heard something in his earbud and slowed to a stop, holding up his hand to me and Bobby Sparks.

"She made a call about eleven minutes ago," he said, looking up at a clock on the station wall. It was 6:36, which put the call at 6:25.

Bobby Sparks grumbled, "It took us eleven minutes to—"

"I can't control the National Security Agency," Mahoney snapped, cutting him off. "In the call, an unidentified female said in Arabic: 'Why?' Unsub male replied in Arabic: 'Four and zero.' End of conversation. We have a rough idea of unsub male's location: not far from where Suitland Parkway meets the Anacostia Freeway."

"He could be coming toward us," I said, looking at the clock.

"Possibly," Mahoney agreed, and he started to move again.

"'Four and zero,'" I said. "What did the unsub male say the first time?"

"'One, four, and zero,'" Bobby Sparks replied.

"How long ago was that?"

"Just after she entered the station," Mahoney said. "It was at five twenty-five."

"So they dropped the one, and an hour has passed," I said.

Both FBI agents slowed. "Again," Bobby Sparks said.

"An hour and forty from five twenty-five is seven oh-five," I said. "Forty minutes from six twenty-five is seven oh-five. I think we've got their timetable."

Mahoney paled. "Which means we've got less than twenty-nine minutes to find her."

CHAPTER

59

IT TOOK HALA A GOOD TWENTY SECONDS BEFORE SHE COULD GET HER MUSCLES to relax and her eyes to open. She gritted her teeth at the burning pain in her hip as she looked all around her.

To her left and down the tracks, red lights glowed at intervals all the way to the snow-blanketed mouth of the terminal. Hala could make out, about fifty feet ahead of her, the dark hulks of the suburban MARC trains. She smelled diesel exhaust and heard the rumble of the Acela's engines warming and the chatter of the last few grateful travelers boarding the train bound for New York City.

Hala got out her phone and checked the time: 6:47 p.m. She had eighteen minutes to get into position and get ready. Limping toward the far end of the dark commuter train, she heard the Acela's wheels begin to squeal across the tracks, pushing north.

She stood in the darkest shadows, feeling the effects of the painkillers start to seep through her as she ripped open the first of the Christmas presents and watched the train leave the terminal. Weary travelers were visible in the lit windows.

Hala wondered if these train passengers would look back on this day and feel the way people who'd been late to work at the World Trade Center on 9/11 did: confused and haunted by the random circumstances that had led to their survival.

SEEING THAT THE GRATE ABOVE THE STALL IN THE MEN'S RESTROOM HAD NO screws holding it to the wall, I stepped up on the toilet and yanked at it. It was exactly 6:57. It had taken us that long to clear the restroom and search it.

The grate didn't budge. I used Mahoney's flashlight and shone it through the slats before looking back at him, Bobby Sparks, and Captain Johnson. "Where do these ducts go?" I asked Johnson.

The Amtrak cop squinted at me in disbelief. "You think she got in there?"

"I don't know how else to explain that the grate's been wired shut from inside. So where do they go?"

Johnson looked confused. "I don't know. And I don't think there's anyone from maintenance who can tell us until—"

"Wait, why don't you know this?" Bobby Sparks asked incredulously.

"We control the gate areas and the tracks," the Amtrak cop retorted hotly. "The station's interior is the responsibility of a private management firm in Virginia, but everyone there's got the night off. It's Christmas, for God's sake."

I gestured angrily at the duct. "Where *could* it go? Or, better, what places would be vented by this ductwork?"

Captain Johnson thought a second, said, "Sbarro, the pizza place that's around the corner here, and then the U.S. Postal Service facility, I guess."

"How big is that?" Bobby Sparks asked.

"Big enough to handle everything coming off Capitol Hill, House and Senate side, and all the federal agencies around here."

"There's no chance anyone from the U.S. Postal Service is working on Christmas," Mahoney said.

"As a matter of fact, there's a skeleton crew in there right now," Johnson said. "I saw them on the loading dock. They're on until ten."

I thought about that a second, then said, "Does the loading dock face First Street or the terminal?"

"Both," the Amtrak officer said. "There's a single steel roll-up door facing the street, and a double that allows access to the tracks."

"She's either escaping to the street or trying to get to the trains," I said, moving toward the door. "Get men to the west end of that terminal, inside and outside. Tell them she's dressed as a male, an Amtrak worker, and should be considered armed and dangerous."

Captain Johnson began to sweat again as he barked orders into his radio. So did Mahoney and Bobby Sparks and I as we all sprinted to the security entrance that led down to the terminal, the loading platforms, and the train tracks.

61

FEWER THAN FOUR MILES TO THE SOUTH, ACROSS THE RIVER IN ANACOSTIA, A white panel van sporting a sign that said CSX TRANSIT SUPPORT crept through the snow toward the Eleventh Street bridge, heading north into Washington.

The driver was dressed in work boots, a blue one-piece work suit similar to the one Hala wore, and a dark blue insulated Carhartt coat. There was a patch on the chest of the coat that said CSX MAINTENANCE SERVICES. Below that patch, the name HERB had been embroidered.

His real name was Omar Nazad, but he carried the Maryland driver's license and employee ID of Herbert Montenegro of Falls Church, Virginia. A Tunisian who looked more Eastern European than Maghrebian, Nazad had entered the United States on a student visa to study for his doctorate in chemical engineering at Purdue University. But he had left the school almost immediately, disappearing into this new identity courtesy of Al Ayla and Hala Al Dossari.

They'd met six months before in a safe house run by a theater major at Syracuse University. Hala was older than Nazad by almost ten years, but she captivated him with her beauty and her passion for the cause. This plan had been their idea, conceived during the long, wet upstate New York spring and expanded and refined during the summer and early fall. Tonight they and the others would see it through, no matter the consequences.

"Brother?" came a male voice from behind Nazad, back in the interior of the van, which was dark but for the glow of a computer screen.

"I hear you, brother," Nazad answered.

"Six minutes," the man replied.

"We'll just make—" Nazad stopped, cursed.

"What is wrong?"

"Police ahead. They've blocked off the left lane to the bridge. Quiet now."

Nazad pulled shut dark drapes that separated the front seats from the van's rear. He rolled slowly by a police officer waving a flashlight.

"Officer," he called. "Is the exit plowed down onto Twelfth Street? I have to check the tracks as it enters the tunnel."

"Exit's plowed, but nothing beyond it," the officer replied. "Hope you've got chains. It's a mess down in there."

"I take my chances," Nazad said, and drove on.

62

THE PAINKILLERS HAD KICKED IN. HALA POCKETED THE SPOOL OF THIN, ultra-strong fly-fishing tippet line, picked up the tool bag, and limped in the dark shadows on the other side of the suburban MARC trains, heading toward two longer Amtrak trains that were sitting dead and barely lit in the middle of the huge terminal.

She heard screeching and rumbling at the east end of the station. A freight train was leaving the First Street tunnel, which ran under Capitol Hill toward the CSX tracks and the Navy Yard. She felt a thrill go through her at the idea that this might all proceed according to plan, snow delay or not.

Hala made it to the northernmost end of the first dead Amtrak train, more than one hundred and fifty yards from the U.S. Postal Service loading dock. She rested for a second against the snub nose of the massive locomotive, watching the last few cars in the freight train disappear through the terminal mouth, heading toward the Ivy City Yard that was somewhere out there in the snowy darkness. Another train approached the station now.

The Crescent, bound for Atlanta and the Big Easy, Hala thought, feeling the narcotic buzz building and a moment of regret that she would never get to see where jazz was born. Still, she was alert enough to know she needed to duck beneath one of the locomotives so she would not be caught in the southbound train's headlamp.

At 7:02:46, according to her phone, Hala thought she heard something above the din of the approaching train. Crawling to her right, she peered along the platform, catching glimpses of men with guns way back toward the security gates, maybe ten of them, all spreading out and moving east and west of her location. Was that Cross with them? She couldn't tell for sure. Were they on to her? They had to be. They were going toward the MARC trains and the postal facility.

It was 7:03:10 now.

The southbound Crescent squealed into the bay between the F and G loading platforms. There were hardly any people on board, at least not in the rear cars. But after all, it was Christmas night.

Hala crawled back to the tool kit and fished out two of the remaining seven hand grenades, nestled like eggs in the ripped Christmas paper. She held them, looked up at the giant steel roof supports high overhead, and prayed that the infidels would not set off one of her booby traps before it was time.

CHAPTER

63

WE REACHED THE U.S. POSTAL SERVICE LOADING DOCK WITH JUST OVER A minute to spare. Bobby Sparks took one look at the three dead bodies and signaled his men that they should spread out again, move north and east through the terminal, and get to hunting.

Captain Johnson, rattled by the sight of the bodies, called over his radio to tell his men to guard the rear platform while the FBI team went to work. Mahoney and I climbed up on the loading dock. A small television, a portable device probably belonging to one of the postal workers, sat on an overturned crate. It was playing the local news, which had been delayed by the Lions football game, and the broadcast featured a recap of the hostage crisis in Georgetown.

The video showed Henry Fowler in cuffs and leg chains. Fowler's former wife was climbing into the back of an ambulance with her new husband. I was being interviewed by some newswoman. Below me it said:

DC DETECTIVE ALEX CROSS
GEORGETOWN HOSTAGE-CRISIS HERO

I shut the TV off, then noticed my reflection in a window. I sure as hell didn't look like a hero. My hair was wet and I had some ugly stubble on my face. My clothes were soaked with perspiration, and my eyes were red with fatigue.

I had noticed on the news report that my hands were shaking a little and that I kept swallowing hard as I spoke. I also looked unpleasantly thin—not the trimness of a healthy person, but the gaunt, haggard look of a guy who was living life way too hard.

The Fowler situation had wrapped up less than twelve hours ago. Right then, it felt to me like it had happened thirty years ago. Tonight was turning into a much, much bigger nightmare. That was as plain as the bodies of the dead postal workers. Seeing the way their corpses lay broke me out of my thoughts. I did some quick trajectory calculations and then looked up the east wall and saw the gaping hole of the ventilation system.

How in the hell had she—?

Mahoney showed me his watch: 7:04:50. Mahoney said, "We're—"

To the right and not far beyond the railcar the postal workers had been filling, I caught a brilliant flash followed by a stunning explosion. Shock waves hit me, hot metal whizzed by my head, and I dove for the ground.

64

TEN SECONDS TOO SOON, BUT NOT A DISASTER, NOT A GAME CHANGER, HALA thought after she heard the blast—the bomb she'd set closest to the front of that railcar at the loading dock.

Hala heard people yelling as she bit down on the steel clip that ran through the grenade's safety mechanism. She pulled the device away from her, spit out the clip, held the firing lever tight. Wanting to keep them convinced as long as possible that she was attacking from the terminal's west end, Hala leaned back and hurled the grenade up and over the nearest MARC train; she heard it hit and clatter well back by the rear platform.

She ducked behind the front end of the locomotive, head down, protecting her ears and eyes from the blast that shook the terminal. She waited for a count of four, to let any flying debris land, and then threw a second grenade toward the engine of the dark commuter train. It landed on the roof.

Hala was already running east toward the Crescent when that grenade blew. Gun in one hand, tool bag in the other, she fed ravenously on the adrenaline coursing through her, hardly feeling the torn muscle in her hip at all.

65

"UNION TERMINAL IS UNDER ATTACK," I HEARD CAPTAIN JOHNSON YELL INTO his radio after the first explosion. "Stop all incoming traffic. I repeat, shut all rail traffic in vicinity of—"

Another voice bellowed, "Man down!" I scrambled to my feet and looked out through the loading dock door. Special Agent Bobby Sparks was sprawled bleeding and unmoving between the rail tracks. Two of his men were already tending to him.

"Where the fuck is she?" Mahoney hissed at me just before the second blast went off, to our right, on the other side of the closest commuter train. A third explosion flashed and thundered off the top of one of the locomotives.

Out beyond Bobby Sparks and the men working on him, two HRT operators crouched and ran toward the latest explosion, automatic weapons leading. Three Amtrak police officers paralleled them, pistols drawn, leaving the rear platform, moving north onto the loading platform between the MARC trains.

I was looking at the fallen HRT leader, wondering where Hala could have thrown the grenade from, when Mahoney seemed to sense something. "Trap."

"What?"

"Booby traps," he said. "She's drawing..." He shouted into his radio: "HRT, stand your—"

The hostage rescue operator closest to the commuter train broke a delicate fishing line and set off the fourth grenade. He was killed instantly, and his partner seriously wounded, a split second before the fifth bomb went off, between the two commuter trains where the Amtrak police officers had gone.

66

TWO MINUTES BEFORE THE FIRST GRENADE WENT OFF INSIDE UNION STATION
terminal, Omar Nazad fishtailed the van in the deep wet
snow clogging Twelfth Street where it crossed over Water
Street and began to drop toward M Street.

The Tunisian knew from prior trips to the area that
there was a construction site beneath the elevated freeway to his immediate left, an office building that held
community college classrooms on his right, and beyond
that, at M Street, a second office building that was headquarters to some kind of marine engineering company.
But it all looked completely different now, blanketed in
snow, the buildings dark and deserted. It would be one of
the last parts of the city to see a plow.

This was both a blessing and a curse.

At the bottom of the ramp, the snow had drifted so

deep that the van bogged down, and his men had to jump out the back and push.

"One minute fifty!" one of his accomplices called from the van's rear.

"If God wills it, we'll make it, brother," Nazad said between gritted teeth that he clenched tighter when his tires caught and they began to move once more.

Approaching the engineering firm, they almost got stuck again, but he threw the van in low gear and kept it moving, and they slid sideways out onto M Street. The Tunisian could see nothing to his right, but he knew that somewhere there in the darkness was the incomplete infrastructure of a ramp that would eventually connect the Eleventh Street bridge with the Southeast Freeway. Beneath it was all manner of earthmoving equipment, cranes and the like.

It was in there, into that construction site, that Nazad needed to go, as deep into it as he dared. But the place was buried under seventeen inches of snow, and if he parked on M, the van would mostly likely be seen.

And they'd be questioned.

And that would not do.

"One minute!"

Nazad looked in his rearview, saw no cars; looked out his windshield and saw nothing but the glow of street-lamps on the falling snow. Something Hala had once said echoed in his mind: *In times of crisis, Allah rewards the bold.*

That's when he saw how he might get close to where he needed to be.

"Fifty seconds!"

The Tunisian pulled the van hard to the left, almost up against the median strip that divided M Street in that part of the city. Then he threw the vehicle in reverse, tore back the drapes, and yelled at his men to open the rear door so he could see. The second the door opened, he stomped on the gas.

With all the combined weight in the rear of the vehicle, the van accelerated much faster than Nazad thought it would. It blasted through a cut in the curb that the freeway builders had made and bounded up onto the raised dirt road that ran back into the construction site. Wind had blown the snow around quite a bit here, causing it to drift up against the machines: two backhoes, a dump truck, and a bulldozer. But there was little more than six inches of it on the dirt road.

Praise Allah! the Tunisian thought as they plowed deeper and deeper into the site, so close he could see a few lights on the Southeast Freeway, and then a stronger light, coming nearer. The van stopped.

"Twenty-five seconds!"

Nazad flicked off his headlights and sat there a moment, still looking out the open back doors of the van. Panting, sweat pouring off his brow, and smiling like he'd just won the lottery, the Tunisian heard a train whistle blow and saw, down a steep bank, on the other side of a chain-link fence, the headlight of a locomotive pulling a long line of boxcars toward the entrance to a tunnel that bent to the right at First Street and ran beneath Capitol Hill to Union Station and all points north.

"Count them!" he ordered.

He heard his men counting the boxcars as they passed. Nazad spotted the twenty-ninth car, a green C. Itoh shipping container, just before the snowy night was cut by the wailing of brakes and the screeching of steel wheels on the rails. The entire train came to a slow, mournful halt.

The green container car was less than one hundred feet away.

The Tunisian's face blossomed into another joyous grin and he pounded the wheel of the car. She'd done it! That crazy Hala had done it!

"Out!" he cried to the men in the rear of the van. "Everyone out!"

CHAPTER

67

"SEND AMBULANCES TO THE U.S. POSTAL SERVICE LOADING DOCK ON FIRST Street," Mahoney shouted into his radio. "We've got seven dead, three wounded. Suspect remains at large inside the Amtrak terminal, which has been booby-trapped. I want this place surrounded and as many bomb squads as you can muster. In the meantime, no one—I repeat, no one—gets in or out of here without my say-so."

I didn't envy my old friend that night. Mahoney had been sitting on Union Station with a full HRT team for more than twenty-four hours. He and Bobby Sparks were supposed to have stopped Hala Al Dossari from bombing the station, and now one of the most highly trained agents in the FBI was dead.

Then I remembered something I'd read in the dossier on Hala Al Dossari.

"Dogs," I said to Mahoney. "I'm calling in the K-Nine patrols."

The FBI agent nodded. "Good idea. We've got her boots and jacket. That's enough to key them on her."

"I want them for another reason as well. Hala's afraid of them. Pathologically afraid of them, evidently."

As Amtrak and Metro police set up protective lines around the dead, I wondered whether the random poisoning, the shootings on the loading dock, and the five explosions would be the full extent of the attack. Was that all, or was there more to come, some bigger weapon we hadn't seen yet?

Before I could evaluate that possibility, my frazzled attention turned toward the remaining FBI HRT operators, who were using powerful headlamps and flashlights to search the immediate area for other trip wires.

Yawning, desperate for caffeine, I thought, *Is this what Hala wants? To have the people hunting her feel like they're the hunted?*

I was fairly confident that that was indeed the idea, or at least part of it.

But I could not stop the nagging feeling that, unless she was bent on a pure suicide mission here, we were missing something, that there was more to this than a fanatical woman with access to cyanide, bullets, and bombs.

68

I WENT UP INTO THE STATION, WHERE PEOPLE WERE FRANTIC, DESPITE THE efforts of officers on hand to calm them. They'd heard explosions. Five of them, and they wanted out. I didn't blame them. A part of me, a very big part of me, wanted out too.

Two husky guys in their early twenties began pushing one of the officers guarding the exit near First Street. The cops grabbed the guys by their shoulders, spoke softly, and calmed them down.

A middle-aged man wearing a fancy black cashmere coat accosted me.

"You're Detective Alex Cross, aren't you?" He asked the question as if he were accusing me of something.

"Yes, I'm Alex Cross."

"Do you by any chance know who I am?"

"Yes, sir. I do. Congressman Richard Holt of Delaware."

"That's right," he said. And then his voice moved into the too-friendly tone of a man running for reelection: "It really is necessary for me to be out of the station in the next thirty minutes. Do you think that can be arranged?"

"Congressman, if I could arrange it, I'd have you and everyone else out of here in the next thirty *seconds,* and I'd be at home in my wife's loving arms."

"Excellent," said the congressman. "How long?"

Typical politician. Only listened to himself.

"Mr. Holt," I said. "Read my lips. I would *like* to have you out of here in the next half hour, but that doesn't mean it's going to happen."

Holt smiled a standard candidate's smile and said, "If anyone can do it, you can. After all, you're Alex Cross."

"Doesn't seem to be impressing many people these days," I said as I turned and walked away.

Yeah, I was Alex Cross…without a lead, without a clue, without Hala.

And everywhere I looked, there were angry, frightened people trying to get their needs met:

"My little boy has medication he has to take."

"My cell phone isn't getting any reception. What is this, Nazi Germany?"

"This is exactly the kind of shit I expect from the Metro police. You guys hate black people. You hate us."

"Just stay calm, dear. There's nothing we can do."

"That's always your stupid advice, Barbara. Stay calm. Just stay calm."

I rubbed my temples, tried to find a place of quiet, a moment of sanity, so I could call home again.

Nana answered on the first ring. "You coming home, Alex?"

"Soon as I'm able."

"You okay?"

"I am. I just wanted you all to know that. Bree there?"

"She and Jannie have gone to the corner for milk and eggs."

"I'll try her cell."

"You be safe now," my grandmother said. She paused, and then added in a worried tone, "Alex, I don't feel good about whatever you're doing."

"Having visions these days?"

"I'm telling you what I am feeling," she said, hurt. "What we're all feeling."

I hesitated, willing myself not to fall into the trap of thinking too much beyond the task at hand. When someone is lobbing grenades, you want to be single-minded, even if it hurts the people closest to you.

"I promise you I'll be safe, Nana," I said at last. "And I'll call again when we've wrapped this up and I'm coming home."

"Please do that, Alex. I mean, come home."

"Always," I said, and I hung up.

CHAPTER

69

SNOW BEGAN TO FALL AGAIN AS ONE OF NAZAD'S MEN SET DOWN HIS BOLT cutters after clipping out an entire section of the chain-link fence that separated them from the train tracks. He and the other two members of the Family were all wearing the same fake CSX repairman uniforms as their leader.

"Get the substitute barrels," Nazad hissed to two of them, and he told the third, "Bring the tank."

The Tunisian charged down the steep bank in the knee-deep snow as the flakes grew thicker and fell faster until it was almost as if he were in one of those Christmas movies that the infidels so adored and he so despised. Almost there, he glanced to his left along the boxcars. He was unable to see the two locomotives at the head of the freight train, which was good: he wanted them deep inside the tunnel, blind to what was about to happen twenty-nine cars back.

He reached the green C. Itoh container car and went to its rear doors, which were locked. To ensure the integrity of the cargo, whoever had loaded the car had sealed the locks with heavy-gauge steel cables and crimped metal plates that bore the date and time the doors were closed.

One of Nazad's men appeared, lugging what looked like a scuba tank. Nazad reached inside his coat and pulled out an apparatus that included two rubber hoses, a brass connector, and the thin neck and head of an acetylene torch.

They had it attached in seconds. Nazad glanced up the north bank toward the freeway. No one would ever see them down here. Who would look anywhere but the road in a crazy storm like this?

He got out a flint striker, turned the gas on, and lit the torch with a sound like a cork popping. With three slow, deliberate slashes, he severed the cables from the sealing plates. They fell, hissing, into the snow at his feet.

Nazad shut the torch off and handed it to his helper, who set it aside and started to claw his way back up through the snow toward the repair van. Nazad retrieved the sealing plates and pocketed them. It was snowing so hard now that he kept blinking at the infernal flakes as he opened the door.

"Brother," he heard one of his men say with a gasp. "It is too much!"

The Tunisian grimaced, looked around the door, and saw the other two men with him at the bottom of the bank, a blue fifty-five-gallon drum half submerged in the snow between them.

"We can't lift it!" the other man said. "Without the snow, yes, we could use the dolly, but it's too much."

Nazad lost it. Livid, he ran to them, down the path that had begun to form. "Too much?" he said, slapping one man and then the other. "It's too much for you to get six barrels one hundred feet through the snow, and not too much for Hala to risk her life to stop this train for you? Think of where she is, brothers. Think of what she's doing for you and for Allah right now."

70

HALA SHIFTED UNCOMFORTABLY. HER HIP WAS THROBBING AGAIN, AND SHE'D just taken another painkiller, since she'd been forced to adopt an incredibly awkward position in order to remain up on the axle housing of the rear passenger car of the Crescent.

Melting snow and water dripped all around her. The axle itself was greasy and slick, and it stank of oil. But the metal was surprisingly warm, and she'd been able to straddle the axle, the gun and the tool bag stuffed on a flange above her. She held tight to what looked like part of the brake.

They might come and shine their lights up under each carriage, she thought. But that would take awhile, certainly long enough for Nazad and his men to complete their part of the mission. She could almost hear Alex

Cross and the FBI men thinking, *She's booby-trapped the place. Who knows how many devices she's set up?*

They would be slow now, methodical. Hala closed her eyes, praying that Nazad and his men would have enough time.

71

NAZAD AND THE THREE OTHER MEN STRAINED AGAINST TWO NYLON STRAPS HE'D wrapped around the second barrel that had come down from the truck. They pulled the heavy, awkward load over snow that was becoming packed down and more navigable despite the flakes still falling all around them.

Grunting, they made one last heave, slid the barrel up against the green railcar, and tipped it upright. It had to weigh three hundred pounds, at least.

"Third one comes out first," the Tunisian said with a gasp as he climbed up onto the buckles that held the train cars together and then up over the transom into the container itself. He flipped on a headlamp and saw three blue barrels that looked almost exactly like the substitutes he'd brought to the door. They were sitting up on a pallet.

Each barrel had a plastic sleeve glued to its side that

held documents identifying its manufacturer as Pinkler Industries, and its contents as organophosphates. Nazad carefully stripped the sleeve label off the far right barrel, set it aside, and then, together with his men, muscled the barrel to the door. They wrapped the nylon moving straps beneath the barrel and then eased it out of the container car, two men holding the straps, two men guiding the barrel down.

When they had it sitting upright beside the container, Nazad said, "Hurry. We rest when we are finished."

In seconds they had the straps beneath the first substitute barrel from the van, and then they reversed the process and loaded it inside. Feeling like he'd soaked his clothes with sweat despite the cold weather, the Tunisian nevertheless pushed on, dancing the replacement barrel up beside the two on the pallet. He got out glue, smeared it on the back of the plastic sleeve, and affixed the sleeve to the substitute barrel.

And so it went, Nazad and his men moving each barrel loaded with organophosphates out of the railcar and putting in its place a look-alike barrel filled with sand. With the lading documents attached to the containers, no one would figure out the organophosphates were missing until it was far too late.

Nazad gestured with his chin toward a cardboard box at the rear of the pallet and said, "Take that one too. Then we'll lock up and leave."

One of the men picked it up with a grunt and waddled toward the door.

The Tunisian checked his watch. They'd been working

nonstop for almost an hour and a half. *Hala had done the impossible,* he thought. *Hala had stood up for God, and the One had rewarded her for her boldness, rewarded all of them for their boldness. Their purpose was, clearly, a sacred—*

The light nearly blinded him.

"What the hell's going on in here?" a man's voice demanded in English. "And who the hell are you?"

72

"CAN YOU GET HIM TO SPEAK WHEN WE GET IN THERE?" I ASKED JENNIFER Carstensen, the officer who handled Jasper, a huge white German shepherd. Jasper was one of three police dogs who, along with their human partners, had responded to my call, the officers leaving their homes and families on Christmas to help us track down a terrorist.

We were on the stairs that led down to the terminal. Above us, people who an hour before had been standing in line frantic to get tickets were now standing in line frantic to be released from the station.

"We can absolutely get Jasper to speak," Officer Carstensen replied. "He's been taught to vocalize an alert bark, an attack bark, and a gathering howl. Which one do you want?"

Jasper panted with excitement. He could tell a hunt was about to begin. With every breath the dog took, his powerful shoulder and neck muscles rippled. It almost felt unfair to turn a beast like Jasper loose on someone who was deathly afraid of dogs.

But Hala Al Dossari had killed seven people, two of them FBI HRT specialists. *Unfair* did not even begin to describe the lengths we'd take to apprehend her and make her face justice. We had the terminal surrounded. We had also sealed off the opening into the Ivy City Yard and the First Street tunnel. We had two bomb teams on hand as well, one Metro DC Police, the other FBI. And we had Jasper and his two eager pals.

"I want him howling," I told Officer Carstensen. "I want all three of them howling like a pack of wolves when it's time."

"Ready and waiting, Alex," she said, and she slipped Jasper a treat.

"Al Dossari really that scared of pooches?" Mahoney asked.

"I'm counting on it," I said.

An ironic smirk appeared on his face. "You know, Alex, what you're about to do could be construed as psychological coercion."

"Torture?" I replied skeptically. "No. This is just a way to flush her out quicker and prevent further bloodshed."

"Exactly," Mahoney said.

I was too damn tired to argue the point. "We ready, Ned?"

"Five minutes," Mahoney said. "Bomb squads are moving into final position at the east and west ends of the terminal."

I glanced at my watch. Half past eight. With luck, this would all go smoothly, and I'd get home in time to kiss my wife good night before Bree put on her kerchief and I put on my cap and both of us settled down for a long winter's nap.

FOR A SECOND, WITH THE BRILLIANT LIGHT SHINING IN HIS EYES, AND THE commanding voice of a stranger he could not see ringing in his ears, Omar Nazad felt bewildered, foiled, perhaps a martyr for nothing.

Where had the man come from? Who was he? Police?

Then training took over. He and Hala had gamed almost every scenario, including being spotted in or around the train.

"CSX Nashville asked us to check on this shipment," Nazad said, holding his hand up to block the light, seeing the silhouette of a burly man standing in the doorway. "Could you put that down?"

The light was directed down, and the Tunisian saw a bearded male in his late forties wearing a snowy CSX coat not that dissimilar from his own. The rail worker held a flashlight in one hand, a radio in the other.

"We didn't get no call about a shipment check," the man said, scowling.

"The storm," Nazad said, walking casually toward him. "It has affected everyone. Everything. Can you believe they make us work in this shit?"

The man seemed to relax, asked, "Where you out of?"

"Benning Yard," Nazad said, referring to the local CSX rail maintenance facility. He glanced at footprints behind the man and saw that he'd come down the opposite side of the train, from the direction of the tunnel.

The real CSX employee scrunched up his nose. "They sent a mechanic to do a cargo check?"

The Tunisian smiled like they were allies. "In times of crisis, my friend, each man must do his part. Is that not true?"

The CSX man scratched at his beard, said, "Guess so. Hell, what's in there they got you out in the middle of a blizzard?"

"A potentially unstable chemical," Nazad said. "But I have checked the shipment. Everything is fine. Quite stable."

The man's eyes shifted from the Tunisian, drifted across the floor of the container, focused on the cut plastic strapping that had held the three drums together on the wooden pallet. He said, "No problem. Lemme just check on this. What's your name?"

"Herb," Nazad said. "Herb Montenegro."

The man nodded, raised his radio, clicked Transmit, and managed to say, "Tony, you by the channel?" before the steel toe of Nazad's boot viciously connected with his windpipe, crushing it.

The rail worker choked. Eyes bugging out, he dropped the radio and the flashlight, reached for his throat, and then crumpled to his hands and knees, fighting for air. Nazad jumped out of the container, landed square on the man's back, and drove him face-first into the deep snow, making sure he would never be by the channel again.

From somewhere in the snow next to the suffocating man, the Tunisian heard a voice with a Boston accent say, "This is Tony. How the hell's it looking back there?"

74

HALA STILL STRADDLED THE AXLE OF THE RAILCAR. THE DRIPPING FROM the underside of the train had all but stopped, but she shivered in the north breeze coming into the terminal from the Ivy City Yard and against the greasy steel that had gone cold beneath her. Though her fingers and toes stung, she was somewhat grateful for the cold; it had penetrated her pelvis and calmed her hip as much as the drugs.

But would she be able to run if she had to? Fight if she had to?

Despite the narcotics, Hala knew, she was still mentally able to fight, and she still had three grenades and twenty-five more rounds for the pistol. But would she be able to move the way she needed to if—

The howls rose from behind her, at the station, some-where on the terminal's rear dock: one, two, and then three; left, right, and center. The baying triggered an involuntary shudder that rolled through Hala head to toe and instantly hurled her back in time.

She saw herself at four, at her grandfather's place in the desert, petrified by a pack of wild dogs that were tearing into a young goat that had gotten out beyond the fence. Horrified and angry, Hala had gone to help the goat. The dogs turned on her, mauled her legs and arms, tried to kill her.

Twenty-nine years later, hiding beneath the train and listening to the police dogs howling, Hala was enveloped by the same terror she'd felt when the pack in Saudi Arabia had tried to tear her limb from limb. Shaking now, sweating, she had to use everything in her power to keep herself from collapsing and curling into the fetal position.

A voice in Hala's mind, her late husband's voice, told her she had to fight. She could kill the first dog, and maybe the first dog's handler. But the police that followed them? And the second dog? And the third?

Despite Tariq's voice commanding Hala to focus and figure out a way to escape the dogs and join Nazad, she kept thinking about that baby goat from her childhood, how it had bleated in fear as the pack circled and snapped at its legs. She kept seeing the dogs turn on her, feeling their teeth ripping at her skin.

Hala fought off the urge to puke and shook her head, willing herself to conquer a fear that felt primitive and instinctual.

The howling stopped. She gasped, feeling smashed up

inside and somewhat embittered at the method Allah had fashioned for her martyrdom.

My greatest fear becomes my sacrifice? My deliverance?

"Hala Al Dossari." A voice that echoed through the terminal came from the public address system high overhead. "This is Alex Cross with Metro DC Police. You are surrounded. You have no chance of escape. And we have your jacket and boots from the ventilation duct. You have one minute to lay down your weapons and reveal yourself." A long pause. "Or we'll release the dogs."

Cornered, up against the wall, she considered giving up, surrendering herself so Nazad and the others could complete their mission and put Al Ayla, the Family, at the front of the fight against the great Satan. She might not share in the blessed experience, but she would live to hear about these great things. She would live to rejoice at God's will on earth.

Or she could buy Nazad even more time. He had not yet called her or texted her to say the transfer had been completed. And it was still snowing, was it not? It was. Her duty, her obligation, was to the overall mission.

Hala made herself slide down off the axle, forced herself to go back once more to that day when she was four and the dogs had tried to kill her. In her mind, she rewound the tape of the attack, finding her little-girl self watching the baby goat die, and feeling an injustice and a rage like no other begin to boil.

If they send dogs, she thought, *then dogs will die.*

75

"ROBBY? YOU BY THE CHANNEL?"

Frantically, Nazad dug in the snow around the rail worker.

"Robby?"

"Brother?"

The Tunisian looked back and saw the three other Family men, eyes wide at the sight of the body. "Not now," he barked, feeling something in the snow.

An antenna!

The Tunisian jerked it up, brought the radio to his lips, triggered Transmit, coughed, went nasal, and said, "Dropped the goddamned radio in the snow and I think I'm coming down with a frickin' cold. Come back."

"We got Nyquil and other stuff in the locomotive cab up here. Ice building on them rails?"

"Nothing to worry about," Nazad said.

"You better start heading this way, then," Tony said. "Union Station's saying we might be able to move along here at some point."

"They say what's going on?"

"Some nut's loose in the station, but they're bringing in dogs after her."

Dogs? Nazad flashed on Hala, begged Allah to have mercy on her, and then responded, "Be right along. Fast as I can get through this snow."

The Tunisian stuck the radio in his coat, looked at the three men. One said, "Everything is in the van, brother. We are good?"

Nazad thought about that, shook his head, pointed at the other two men and then the dead body. "Bury this one in the snow on the other side of the tracks, where he won't be seen from the freeway when it melts."

He looked back to the third man. "You come with me, Aman."

"Where are we going, brother?" Aman asked, confused.

Nazad said, "To see this Tony who drives the train before he comes looking for his friend."

76

THE SECOND HAND ON MY WATCH SWEPT PAST TWELVE. A MINUTE HAD elapsed.

"Her call," I said, and then I nodded to Mahoney, who spoke into his radio and ordered the dog team at the far west end to pick up her scent.

From my position midterminal on the rear platform, facing the locomotive for the Crescent train, I saw a rott-weiler, as dark as Jasper was white, leap off the postal loading dock on a leash. His handler let him sniff the jacket and boots Hala had left in the ventilator duct.

Flanked by FBI HRT personnel, three to a side, the dog started to arc northwest and quickly disappeared from my view. I looked to Officer Carstensen, who was stroking Jasper's head.

"Will we know when he's got the scent?" I asked.

Before she had time to answer, an excited howl rose and then broke into baying.

"That Pablo's a good dog," Carstensen said.

I picked up the microphone that connected me to the terminal's public address system and said, "Can you hear him, Hala? His name is Pablo. He smells you. You can't see him yet, but that dog's salivating, wild with the idea of tracking you down. So are the others. There's an absolute monster dog named Jasper here next to me. He's dying to meet you too."

Mahoney looked at me, amused. "You're kind of enjoying that, Alex."

I shrugged. "You always say, if you're gonna do something, do it right."

"Now?" Carstensen said.

"We're following your lead from here on out," I replied.

The K-9 officer listened for the barking of the tracking dog and then gave her animal partner an order I did not understand. But Jasper certainly did. If the dog had been a football player, he'd have been a safety, up on his toes, alert, excited, ready to cut in any direction. Jasper's ears stood straight up, swiveled like mini satellite dishes. He raised and lowered his head, halted, quivered, and then surged against the leash and barked.

"He hears something," Carstensen said.

"You gonna let him go?"

"Didn't you say there could be booby traps?"

I nodded.

"Then I'll be holding him until I get a visual," she said,

gripping Jasper's leash with both hands. You could tell the dog wanted to run. You could also tell Carstensen loved the dog too much to let him. We followed her lead, heading out onto platform F, the Crescent to our left. Amtrak had opened all doors on all trains in the terminal so the dogs could scent-check each car.

Four or five cars along, Jasper paused, listening to the sound of the other two dogs barking in the terminal. Then he nosed around the exit to the sixth car and began progressing at a brisker pace, as if he were ignoring things he knew to be ignorable, moving to his own music.

I don't know if this makes sense, but Jasper seemed so sure of himself that I was confident that Hala Al Dossari was as good as subdued, cuffed, and on her way to the federal lockup across the river in Alexandria.

What the hell was I thinking?

CHAPTER

77

OMAR NAZAD MOVED EASILY IN THE SPACE BETWEEN THE FREIGHT CARS AND the tunnel wall, listening to the dry crunch of the coarse gravel under his boots, such a change from the snow. The soft echoes of Aman's footfalls came to him from the other side of the train. Aman wore a headlamp that glowed a soft red, just enough for him to see the way ahead, not quite strong enough to attract attention.

The Tunisian, however, carried Robby's flashlight and wore the dead rail worker's hat and coat. He wanted to attract attention. He wanted Tony, who he figured was the engineer in the locomotive cab, to be focused on him and how at ease he seemed.

Nazad had no choice in the matter. The original plan had called for leaving the train intact and letting it chug north with the engineers having no idea that the load had been hijacked and substituted. But the dead railroad worker had changed everything. They needed to improvise, make sure that the freight train continued north.

He and Aman kept pace in the tunnel, adjusting to each other when they passed between cars. At last Nazad saw the halo of light thrown from the cab. He did not hesitate but went straight to the ladder and began noisily climbing up the side of the locomotive to the narrow steel platform by the door. A soft light in a metal protective housing glowed above and to the left of the door.

The dead rail worker had had a key card in his pocket, and Nazad had given it to Aman. He prayed the fool of a Turk was climbing quietly. Keeping below the window, he got to the left of the cab door. Nazad reached up, twisted the bulb dark, and then knocked.

"Use your key, for Christ's sake, Robby," a voice yelled back. "I'm pouring us some holiday grog here."

The Tunisian rapped his knuckles on the glass again.

"For Jesus's sake, Robby, I love you, but you're an imbecile sometimes."

He heard a creaking noise and thought he saw a shadow before a pie-faced man wearing a white shirt, Christmas-green suspenders, and a Santa hat appeared in the door window. He was carrying a coffee cup and a fifth of Johnnie Walker, and he peered out with confusion before he flipped some kind of switch or pressed some kind of button.

The door slid back with a sigh. Nazad flipped on the Maglite and swung it and the gun around and into the doorway, expecting to find Tony on the other end of the muzzle. But in the next instant, he realized that the engineer had stepped back and to the right.

The Tunisian also saw that there was a second man in the cab, sitting in front of what looked like the instrument panel of a modern jet airplane. Instinct took over. Nazad began to pivot the pistol toward Tony, yelled, "Down on the—"

But the engineer was too quick for him. With a flick of his wrist, Tony hurled scalding-hot coffee at Nazad's face.

Blinded in one eye, the Tunisian screamed and dropped the gun. The pain was excruciating, far worse than the knee to the stomach and the blow to the back that quickly leveled him. He heard Tony say, "Call Union, Pete. Tell 'em we've got our own nutcase down here. And a man missing."

A whoosh. "Drop the gun, or I blow your brains out!" Aman shouted.

Nazad heard a gun clatter to the floor. He raised his head, looked around with his good eye. Aman stood in the doorway, shaking from head to toe, swinging his pistol from one railroad worker to the other, screaming, "And no one calls anyone!"

78

BENEATH THE LAST CAR ON THE CRESCENT, HALA LISTENED TO THE DOGS baying. She thought of how quickly Cross had identified and attacked her one weakness. She heard the different barks coming at her; it was almost as if they were triangulating in on her. Her mind conjured images of them coming after her, ripping at her skin, and she became totally panic-stricken, crying out to God for mercy and deliverance, and finding none.

The children.

Hala swore she heard Tariq's voice calling to her again. *You must fight for them, Hala.*

It was Tariq's voice. Her dead husband talked to her from beyond the grave. *Fight for our children, Hala.*

The image of her son and daughter surfaced in her drugged and terrorized mind. She saw her children threatened by dogs. In an instant, Hala felt all fear and all pain drain from her, leaving her trembling, blinking, as if her spirit had been slipped back into her body somehow.

The dogs' barking was closer now. The only possible way to freedom was straight ahead, toward the far north end of the terminal and the Ivy City Yard. But she knew she'd be in the open, and she'd probably face dogs and gunfire there as well. It would be a lone martyr's suicide.

Hala would not let that be her fate. If she was going to die, she wanted enemies of God to die along with her. That was the death of a holy warrior. That was the ending she wanted.

Ignoring the dogs, Hala crawled out from under the train car, slammed her back against it, stuffed one grenade in the open top of her blue jumpsuit, and pulled the pins from the remaining two. She saw headlamps cutting to the west. The trackers were almost on her. She heard a bark over her right shoulder, no more than fifty, sixty yards behind her.

Hala whipped the two grenades underhand, one left, one right, both at ninety-degree angles to her position, toward the rottweiler and toward the raised loading platform. Pressing her face against the back of the train car, digging out the pistol and the remaining grenade, Hala felt outside of herself, already spirit, no longer tethered to the husk of her body, an avenging instrument of heaven.

The grenades went off within a second of each other, throwing dust and debris, leaving a caustic smell in the air and making a sound so deafening that for a beat, Hala could hear nothing but the echo of the dog's bark that had come the instant before the first grenade exploded.

The dog had been to her left. Closer than she'd expected. Almost on her.

Fight, Hala.

She saw herself as that little girl going after the dogs with the stick, saw the whole scene as if it were playing on screens all around her.

Hala suddenly threw herself to her left, up to the loading platform and onto her knees, the pistol in her left hand, the grenade in her right.

A female police officer covered in dust knelt next to a whimpering white German shepherd with a growing red stain on its side. Hala's instinct was to shoot the cop and the dog and save the grenade to take as many enemy lives as she could. But then she spotted a large figure crouched in the lingering dust behind the policewoman and the dog.

Alex Cross was aiming a pistol at her.

"Drop it, Hala!" he roared.

"Catch, Cross," Hala said, and lobbed the grenade at him.

I SAW THE GRENADE LEAVE HALA'S HAND AND TURN END OVER END, ITS SAFETY lever flipped, and everything about me seemed over.

My life did not pass before me. I did not see Bree, the kids, Nana, my friends, or my Lord and Savior. There was just the grenade and the end of things somersaulting toward me at last.

I'll never know why my body did what it did then. There was no thought involved, no voice screaming at me to act in a certain way. My only explanation is that my subconscious was hyper-aware of my surroundings, saw things that my conscious self did not. It took control and made me do something approximating a move I'd seen only once, at a jai alai game Sampson had dragged me to in Atlantic City a few years before.

It all seemed to go down in slow motion then, the

way I accepted the grenade with my right hand as if I were catching a fragile egg, the way my feet pivoted hard left, the way my legs uncoiled, hurling my upper body away from Hala, Officer Carstensen, and the wounded dog. My right arm whipped over. My fingers released. The grenade flew fifteen feet into the open door of the train car. I flung myself down on the cement platform, threw my arms up over my head.

I heard a gunshot before the explosion blew out windows on both sides of the Crescent, the sound almost rupturing my eardrums. I felt glass shards slicing into my scalp and hands but knew I had been saved from the brunt of the blast. I lay there no more than a beat before the adrenaline in my body surged again, and with my service pistol leading, I swung myself up into a sitting position, ignoring the tiny streams of blood dripping down my face and off my slick hands.

Hala was gone.

Officer Carstensen lay in her own blood, shot through the right shoulder. She looked at me, dazed, released her hold on Jasper, and gestured weakly with her left hand as she tried to speak. I couldn't hear, but I understood. Hala had rolled backward off the platform the same way she'd rolled on.

Jasper sniffed at the blood on his handler's shirt, got to his feet with his hackles rising, and lunged away from Carstensen. The wounded dog took two bounds and then leaped off the loading platform.

Sound began to return to me, a dull roar, and then ringing, and then the thud of another gunshot, terribly close. The sound of Jasper yipping in pain was followed by the most terrified screams I have ever heard.

These things all brought me to my feet. I jumped from the end of the loading platform, gun drawn, spotting the tracking dog and the HRT operators moving swiftly toward us.

I went down on my knees and aimed the Maglite beam under the railcar, searching for the source of the screaming. Jasper had been shot again, this time in the back leg. I could see broken bone and torn sinew.

But he had Hala pinned on her right side, and she was screaming in Arabic. Jasper had bitten deep into her left biceps and was shaking her as if trying to tear her arm loose from its socket.

80

OMAR NAZAD FOUND ANTIBIOTIC CREAM AND BANDAGES IN THE FREIGHT train's first-aid kit. And he'd eaten a few of those pills Hala had insisted they all carry, so his face and blinded eye throbbed less.

In fact, the Tunisian felt like he was on top of things once more, doing Allah's work, as he sat astride the train engineer, pinning the man's back and shoulders to the floor of the cab. Aman was on the floor as well, bracing Tony's head between his knees and pressing his gun to the engineer's temple.

From the floor, the Tunisian picked up a cup of coffee. It was fresh and scalding hot; he'd just taken it out of the microwave at the back of the cab. He held it with his right hand, feeling warm and fuzzy as he reached toward the engineer's horrified face.

"No! What are you doing?" Tony yelled.

Nazad smiled. "What's that saying from your Old Testament? An eye for an eye?"

"No! Please!" Tony screamed as the Tunisian pried up his right eyelid.

"It's either this or death, infidel," Nazad said, and he poured the boiling-hot coffee onto the engineer's eye, saw it turn gray and then milky as Tony went insane, bucking and screeching out pleas to God and his mother.

Now the Tunisian felt better about losing his sight in one eye, and he got up off the engineer. Tony rolled around, hands covering the wounded eye.

"He needs a hospital," said Pete, the other engineer, who'd watched in shock. "And so do you."

"I need only God's blessing," Nazad snarled. "You take him to the hospital when you finish your trip."

"What?" Pete said.

"What is your destination?" the Tunisian asked.

"New Jersey. Freight yard on the west side of the Hudson."

"When you get there, you may take your friend to the hospital," Nazad said, and then he looked at Aman.

In Arabic, he said, "This is your destiny, brother. You will stay on the train until you reach New Jersey, and then make your escape. Go to the Syracuse house."

Upset, the Turk said, "But that's not the plan. I won't be there to see the blow struck."

"And I lose an eye to see the blow struck," Nazad snapped. "These things are the will of God, brother. The will of God."

Book Three
LEAVING ON A FAST TRAIN

81

THEY RUSHED BOTH OFFICER CARSTENSEN AND JASPER OUT ON STRETCHERS from the Union Station terminal. They took Hala Al Dossari to Captain Johnson's office on a stretcher too that Christmas night. Plastic ties bound her wrists and ankles. Straps pinned her flat to the board. She'd be kept in Johnson's office until the roads were clear enough for the Feds to transfer her.

As the EMTs worked to clean up my cuts, I called home. Bree answered.

"Hey," I said. "It's done. I'm good. Couple nicks, but good. Well, a lot of nicks, but still good."

I heard my wife exhale gently. "That's the best news I've heard all day, Alex. When will you be home?"

"Before midnight," I promised. "Just a few things to take care of now."

"You gonna tell me what happened?"

"Full disclosure," I said. "After I open that present you were telling me about at dinner."

"Hmm," she said, a bit skeptically. "Unless you're a superman, I don't think you'll be ready or able to unwrap something like that tonight."

"There's always tomorrow."

"We're celebrating Boxing Day now?"

"That too. Christmas has twelve days, you know."

She laughed, said, "I love you."

"I love you too. Before you know it, I'll be snoring in bed next to you."

"Perfect," she said, and she hung up.

Eventually, the EMTs finished cleaning and bandaging my cuts. They said I needed to go to a hospital to have the wounds checked by a doctor. Instead, I headed to Captain Johnson's office. Hala was probably still there, but soon the roads would be good enough for her to be transferred; she'd be taken to the Alexandria detention center, where she'd be held until her arraignment in federal court.

The office door opened before I got to the FBI agent guarding it. Mahoney came out of the room, his face flushed. "She won't say a damn thing in English, Alex, and seems to find the entire situation laughable. That's not right. Someone like that's just not right in the head."

"I think there's not a doubt about that," I said.

"Yeah?" Mahoney said. "Well, I've got an idea that just might get her thinking right. I've got to go wake up some important people."

"Mind if I try talking to her in the meantime?"

"They're starting the transfer in five minutes," Mahoney said, distracted. "But sure, go ahead, knock yourself out, Alex."

82

"NORTHBOUND CSX FREIGHT, WE NEED TO GET THAT TUNNEL CLEARED, SO you'll be first out," said the Union Station radio dispatcher, his voice coming over the speaker built into the dash of the locomotive. "You're good to go in five."

Aman pressed the muzzle of his pistol to Pete the engineer's temple. With a shaky hand, Pete triggered the hand mike, said, "Appreciate it. Everyone safe up there?"

"They set the dogs on her; got the bitch."

"Thank God," Pete said.

Omar Nazad wanted to pour scalding coffee into Pete's eye too, but he restrained himself. There was nothing he could do for Hala now but execute the plan, make the great blow himself.

"I leave, then," he said, clapping Aman on the back. "Go with God, brother."

"And you, brother," Aman said.

The Tunisian never bothered to turn his weeping eye toward the other engineer, who sat in the corner moaning with pain.

The cold wind coming up the tunnel was like new fire against the burns on Nazad's cheek, but the bandage blocked it from hitting his eye. Nazad climbed down from the cab as the diesel engines coughed up black smoke through the exhaust stacks. The locomotive began to rumble.

Nazad reached the ground, ate another pain pill, flipped on the Maglite. As the freight train groaned and began to move, the Tunisian started to jog in the opposite direction, toward the tunnel mouth, thinking pleasantly about the present he and his men would soon give to all Americans on Hala Al Dossari's behalf.

I WENT INTO CAPTAIN JOHNSON'S OFFICE, SAW TWO FBI AGENTS I DIDN'T recognize standing on either side of Dr. Al Dossari's stretcher, near a window that overlooked the terminal and the tracks. Hala gazed at me, seeming to feel a mixture of contempt and interest. Facing this woman who lived beyond the pale, whose beliefs and actions were virtually incomprehensible to me, I felt pretty much the same way about her.

"I need a doctor, Cross," she said.

"You are a doctor," I replied.

"Have you not heard? One cannot heal oneself."

"I have heard that. What I don't get is how a doctor becomes a terrorist."

"But you would understand how a doctor becomes a soldier?"

Before I could figure out how to respond to that, I

heard the now familiar sound of train wheels on tracks and watched a freight train emerge from a tunnel at the station's east end and chug toward the Ivy City Yard and points north. Despite the fact that I was talking to a ruthless terrorist, I couldn't help thinking that some degree of normalcy had returned to Union Station.

"What was this all about?" I asked, gesturing out the window. "I mean, was it a spur-of-the-moment thing? Or part of something bigger?"

She studied me, and I noticed her eyes were glassy and her pupils pinpoint. She said, "Spur-of-the-moment. I was in the area, bored on a holiday I don't believe in, and decided to go out and play in the snow."

One of the agents pressed his earbud and then said, "Let them in."

Four U.S. Marshals came into the office, signed the necessary paperwork, and took Hala into their custody.

"Good-bye, Cross," she said as they wheeled her out. "I hope to meet you again."

"Probably sooner than later," I said, and watched her go.

I heard diesel engines starting, looked out the window, and saw the Crescent light up.

"Dr. Cross?"

I turned to find Captain Johnson, who'd stepped up to the window beside me. "I wanted to thank you. Without your bravery—"

"Without a lot of people's bravery, including yours."

"Yeah, I suppose," he said, his eyes watering as he gestured out at the terminal and the trains. "But what if she'd managed to get something big in here? What if it had gone off?"

"We can only guess at that kind of thing, Captain," I said as the last car in the freight train disappeared from sight. "But for now, Christmas goes on."

CHAPTER

84

IF I'D MOVED QUICKER, FOLLOWED HALA AL DOSSARI AND HER ARMED GUARDS out of Union Station, found a taxi or a patrol car to take me back to my family, I might have made it home before midnight.

But Mahoney caught me crossing the main hall. "I need you, Alex."

"No," I said. "I've got to sleep, Ned. I'm a zombie, no help to anyone."

"I'll get you a B-twelve shot," Mahoney said. "Maybe with a kicker of caffeine and sodium benzoate."

"What?"

"You never took a pick-me-up when you were with the Bureau?"

"No. Never did."

"Works like a charm," Mahoney said, sounding like he'd just gotten ten hours of sleep. "We'll take care of you. We'll go to Alexandria, have another chat with Hala Al Dossari."

"I don't think she'll be talking at any point soon. Time in the cell will loosen her up. More than enough time for me to rest and join you tomorrow afternoon, say."

"No *say*, Alex," Mahoney complained. "I've arranged for a little show, something I think is guaranteed to open her up now."

"Okay, then go run your show. I don't need to be there."

"Actually, you do. You'll be the one to tell me if we're going too far."

CHAPTER

85

OMAR NAZAD TURNED OFF THE FLASHLIGHT AND EMERGED FROM THE MOUTH OF the tunnel to find the storm had eased somewhat; there were just a few random flakes now. He waded into the snow, his eye weeping behind the bandage, his burned skin twitching at each contact with the frozen flakes.

Above him on the elevated freeway, more cars were moving, which meant more streets and lanes had been plowed. It was good. It was a blessed thing. As traffic built, they would blend into the traffic, and—

He heard a soft trilling sound, the call of the desert; he smiled and immediately gave a response back. His last two men, Saamad and Mustapha, were fearless Bedouins from the rugged dry mountains of southern Algeria, warriors for God who would not abandon him no matter what.

Even with the one eye, the Tunisian spotted his brothers in arms standing there on the bank, and he struggled up through the snow to them.

"What has happened to you, brother?" Saamad asked. "Where is Aman? Hala?"

"Allah took my eye," Nazad replied, hearing the slight slur in his voice. "But I am happy to give it for our cause. Hala has been captured, but she will never speak of what we will unleash twenty-six days from now. And Aman is on the train and will make sure it gets far away from here before he makes his escape."

"Allahu Akbar," Mustapha said.

"God is great," Nazad agreed. "Now, let's get out of here, brothers."

CHAPTER

86

THE PLOWS HAD BEEN BUSY THE PAST FEW HOURS, PUSHING LANES CLEAR along many of the main routes of the nation's capital. But they'd thrown up huge banks of snow that sealed off driveways and roads and that buried cars, making some streets look like they were lined with odd-shaped igloos.

My right butt cheek was sore from the B_{12} shot, but, as Mahoney had promised, despite almost forty hours with minimal sleep, I felt alert. Mahoney drove, following a plow as it exited the Southeast Freeway onto 295 and took the Eleventh Street bridge to Virginia. It was slow going, but we had as good a driving surface as could be found that night.

"I wonder why she never tried to contact him again," I said.

"Who?"

"The guy she called. The one who was somewhere near the other end of this bridge."

"I dunno. But you'll get the chance to ask her in a few minutes."

Still following the plow, we left the bridge and headed south on the Shepherd Parkway toward 495, Alexandria, and the detention center where they'd taken Hala Al Dossari to be interrogated and to await arraignment.

I checked my watch. Pushing ten thirty. Last night around this time, I had been outside a mansion in Georgetown, trying to get a psychotic to answer the phone. Now I was on my way to watch Mahoney interrogate a sociopath. I felt tired of my profession right then, wondered what it would be like to change, to put a complete end to coming face-to-face with deranged people, to begin seeking out the good, sane folks, and only the good, sane folks.

That caused me to think of Bree and wonder if I should call her to tell her of my likely delay. But what was the point? She had to be almost expecting that by now. The problem was that when other women in my life had finally come to expect my absence, they had gone on to make it permanent, something I was determined would not occur with Bree.

"This absolutely has to happen now?" I asked, yawning.

Mahoney nodded. Up until then, he hadn't been willing to tell me what he planned for Hala Al Dossari, but now he said, "She's tired, confused, in custody, figuring out she's fucked for life, and she's coming down off painkillers. Looks like Oxy, from the blood work they did on her."

I squinted. "You're saying she's a jihadist and a junkie?"

"I don't know about that," Mahoney said. "But she had a bunch of pills with her, including Oxy, antibiotics, and muscle relaxants."

"Like she was expecting to be wounded."

"Or was just being a prepared doctor," Mahoney said.

87

THE VAN'S REAR WHEELS SPUN IN THE SNOW, DIGGING DEEPER AND DEEPER troughs that almost immediately glazed over with ice.

Omar Nazad pounded the wheel, furious, an emotion compounded and turned into homicidal rage by the shooting pains and twitches that had suddenly started all around his blinded eye. They'd been at this solidly for the past hour, trying to get the van free without attracting attention. It was eighty, maybe ninety, yards out to M Street. You could see the snowed-over tracks they'd laid down coming in. But the van hadn't moved more than six feet in that direction since he'd returned from the tunnel.

Saamad and Mustapha were exhausted. He told them to take some of the pills Hala had given them and try again. But even that had not helped. There was nothing they could do really, except...

He jumped out of the van, turned it off, trudged around the back, and said, "We dig our way out."

"With what?" Mustapha grumbled. "Our hands?"

"This is a construction site," Saamad said. "We find shovels!"

"Shovels?" Nazad said scornfully. "I'm hoping bulldozer or backhoe."

The Tunisian went around the construction site and looked in the cabs of the John Deere backhoe loaders and the Cat D6K bulldozer, but he found no keys. However, as he was climbing down off the second backhoe, the Algerians showed up with tools. They'd broken into a shed at the rear of the site and discovered shovels and picks.

At a quarter to twelve, they began to dig the seventy yards to freedom.

88

THE ALEXANDRIA DETENTION CENTER SITS JUST WEST OF THE 495 FREEWAY, A couple of miles from the U.S. federal court and the local office of the American Civil Liberties Union, which monitors this jail, where terrorists are often held awaiting arraignment or trial.

The U.S. Marshals Service contracts with the Alexandria sheriff's office to hold suspected terrorists in custody, which they do incredibly well. It's one of the cleanest, most humane houses of incarceration that I've ever visited.

We found Hala Al Dossari chained by the ankles to a chair in an interrogation room that had the requisite Formica-topped table and one-way mirror with an observation booth behind it. A translator sitting in that booth would interpret anything Hala said in Arabic and report it to us through earbuds we wore. Hala had been cleaned. Her wounds had been treated. Her clothes had been taken for processing. She was dressed in an orange prison jumpsuit that said FEDERAL on the back. Her left arm hung in a sling.

Hala had evidently been acting in a belligerent manner since being taken into custody by the U.S. Marshals. Despite her wounds, she had refused to cooperate with doctors or jail personnel. They had had to forcibly lift and move her through the medical examination and treatment, and then through the body and cavity search conducted at her intake. She'd refused food and water and had to be carried into the interrogation room by two deputies who'd been defensive linemen at Old Dominion.

She ignored Mahoney and focused on me with an expression that revealed neither surprise nor fear.

"We meet again, Cross," she said. "So soon you want to talk? I do not think this is smart for me to do. I want my lawyer."

"Federal public defender's on his way," Mahoney said agreeably. "But it might be awhile. The snowstorm, you know."

"I say nothing to you anyway. So go ahead, we stay here all night."

"I'll arrange that," Mahoney said with a plastic smile, and he left the room, which was what he had told me he was going to do.

I said nothing, just sat down and watched her watching me. It was still hard for me to believe that someone with such intelligence, training, and classic beauty had turned out so ruthless and cold-blooded.

The silence, as I expected, finally unnerved her. "You the good cop?"

"I like to think so, Dr. Al Dossari," I said. "The fair one, at least."

"Fair," she said as if she were spitting the word. "You used dogs on me."

I shrugged. "I knew dogs frightened you. I used it. You would have done the same thing."

She glared at me.

"Why'd you kill your husband?"

"I did not kill him. He killed himself at the order of a crazy man."

"Whom you in turn killed?"

Hala said nothing.

"Your dossier makes interesting reading. And the Saudi embassy has promised to ship over everything it has on you."

"So?"

"So I'm sure I'll find other things in there, ways to get inside your head."

Her chin rose, and she looked down her nose at me as if she were of noble birth and I were a slave. "You could spend every day of the rest of your life studying me, Cross, and you would not come close to an understanding of who I am."

"Some people are inexplicable," I agreed. "But not you, Doctor. You are easy to explain. Even without more information about your shitty childhood or whatever drove you to the Family, I know you will ultimately be defined by your fanaticism. That is how people will understand you, and how they'll condemn you: as an insane doctor, a terrorist willing to poison and bomb innocent people for her own twisted ends."

CHAPTER

89

THE SMILE THAT HALA GAVE ME RAISED THE HAIR ON THE BACK OF MY NECK and almost made me shiver. "I can live with that," she said. "Because I know there are two sides to every story. And I promise you, Cross, for every American who believes your version of events, there will be five Muslims who accept my story: that because of a deep and abiding faith, I decided to live the words of my Prophet and take up arms against the infidels right inside their own center of power. Am I crazy? Or brilliant? Honestly, I don't mind either interpretation."

She didn't. I could see it plain as day in her expression and in the cold tone of her voice. Hala Al Dossari was one of the most disturbing criminals I'd ever tangled with, super-smart but almost reptilian when it came to questions of life and death, able to extinguish a human as easily as she would a bug, as long as it was done in God's name.

"Where have you been the past ten months?" I asked.

"Visiting old friends," she said. "You?"

I ignored the question. "I can help if you let me."

Hala laughed scornfully. "What can you do for me, Cross?"

"Let you see light," I replied.

"I have already seen the light."

"Yes, and that's what will make not seeing the sun so debilitating for you," I said. "You're used to a life spent in powerful sunlight, Dr. Al Dossari. Where you're going, there will be no sunlight, and eventually it will affect your serotonin levels and you'll fall into despair, a state you'll remain in the rest of your life."

She looked at me, blinking but expressionless. "Or?"

"You tell me what this was really about," I said. "What you were really doing inside Union Station."

Hala cocked her head, said, "How many times do I have to tell you, Cross? I was fighting for Allah. It is as simple as—"

The interrogation room door opened. Mahoney returned, carrying a laptop computer with a seventeen-inch screen, and sat beside me. "Any progress?"

"We're establishing a bit of mutual understanding," I said.

"In other words, no," Mahoney said. "Sorry, Alex, but I need to take over the questioning here."

"All yours," I said, and made as if to leave.

Mahoney put his hand on my arm, and I settled back into the chair. Hala shifted uncomfortably in hers.

"I understand you are in pain?" Mahoney said.

She nodded. "I am."

He fished in his jacket pocket, came up with two small white pills, each stamped OC on one side and 10 on the other. He put them on the table where she could see them but not reach them.

90

HALA LOOKED AT THE PILLS, AND I COULD FEEL HER LEG JIGGLING ON THE other side of the table. "So, what? You withhold medical treatment so I talk? I think your ACLU will be interested to hear this."

Mahoney smiled. "Who said anything about withholding treatment?" He slid the tablets over in front of her. "We're not tribal savages a generation out of the desert here."

Hala scowled at him but took up one of the tablets. I pushed a plastic water bottle across the table. She swallowed the painkiller but then said, "If you think I will talk because of these pills, you do not know me."

"Hey," Mahoney said, arms wide: Mr. Nice Guy. "We want to know you, Doctor. We want to hear what you have to say in your defense."

"I'm saying nothing in my defense. I'll wait for the lawyer."

"Let us check a few things that are verifiable," the FBI agent said, as if he were a clerk taking insurance information. "Where do you live in Saudi Arabia?"

Hala did not reply, but she watched him closely.

Mahoney typed on his keypad, rolled his lower lip between fingers, said, "Al Hariq? No, that's where you were born, right out there on the edge of the *erg,* the sea of sand, right?"

He looked up at her. She said, "A place of terrible beauty."

I said, "That where you became afraid of dogs?"

She smiled sourly at me. "I have no idea where that came from. It's always just been there."

"You're smart though," Mahoney observed, returning his attention to the screen. "King Saud University for one year and then four years at Penn, courtesy of the Saudi royal family. Impressive. Medical degree from Dubai. Children. A career. And then a sudden radicalization. But that's what happens when God talks to you, right?"

She said nothing, rolled her eyes at me.

"Now," Mahoney said. "Where do you live in Saudi Arabia?"

"I do not live in Saudi Arabia."

"And probably never will again," the FBI agent said brightly, still looking at his screen. "I guess what I was asking was...oh, here it is. Fahiq. It's right there outside Riyadh, on the road to Mecca."

For the first time since we'd been talking to Hala, I saw

something resembling anxiety in her expression, just a glimpse of it, and then she turned stony once more.

I glanced at Mahoney, who seemed so confident now that I thought, *What has Ned got on her? What about Fahiq could break her?*

CHAPTER

91

"WE NO LONGER LIVE IN FAHIQ," HALA SAID. "WE SOLD THAT HOUSE YEARS ago, long before we came to this—"

"There was a transfer of property," Mahoney agreed. "But it was a gift, not a sale, to Gabir Salmann, who I believe is your uncle, the older brother of your mother, Shada?"

Something shifted in Hala. The coolness was gone. She studied the FBI agent the way a hawk might and made no reply.

"It's right here in the Saudi records the embassy was good enough to send over by courier," he said. "You want to see?"

No answer.

"Despite what you hear, Doctor, the Saudi royal family are, on the whole, keen allies of the United States," Mahoney went on. "Why? They might have all the oil, but we have all the weapons and God only knows how many times the number of soldiers. In any case, the Saudi royals find it most embarrassing when one of their nationals goes off the reservation and starts killing some of the country's best customers and friends."

He paused and looked at me, almost cheery. "Very cooperative, the Saudis." Mahoney held up his hand, set it down, looked back at Hala. "Not a lot of political freedom back home, is there?"

Hala said nothing.

"Not a lot of wiggle room in the judicial system in Saudi, right? Sharia law? Secret police?"

Mahoney leaned forward, began talking louder: "No constitutional guarantees of civil rights and humane treatment. What the Saudi royals want from their people, the Saudi royals get. Am I right, Dr. Al Dossari?"

"So what?" Hala snapped. "I am not in my homeland, and I think there is zero chance that your government extradites me."

"I agree you are not in your homeland, nor are you likely to be any time soon," Mahoney replied. He paused, glanced at me, then said to her, "But your children are there."

I immediately saw a change in her breathing pattern: her respirations became shallow, more rapid. She straightened in her chair.

"What are their names?" Mahoney asked. "Oh, here it is: Fahd, ten, and Aamina, seven. Good-looking kids." He smiled at her. "The last time you spoke to them was when?"

Hala said nothing.

"Got to be ten, eleven months." Mahoney let that hang as he started typing again. "You use Skype, Dr. Al Dossari?"

"No."

"Amazing thing," he said, hitting Return. "You can look right into a compound on the other side of the world."

He slid the computer to his left, where all of us could see it.

Hala took one look and lunged at Mahoney. The chains caught her, but she strained hard against them, and she spit at him before hissing, "Allah will see you in hell for this. And my lawyers will see you in court."

CHAPTER

92

MAHONEY RAISED HIS HAND AND SAID, "YOU'LL NEVER SEE ME IN COURT because there will be no evidence of what you are about to witness, Dr. Al Dossari. And I'll just have to take my chances with Allah."

With my uneasiness building quickly toward horror, I studied the screen: a terrace and part of a beautiful garden where purple and red anemones grew tall and stood floppy in a wide section of grass. There was a table in the foreground with a plate of pastries on it and an icy pitcher of water, or perhaps lemonade. In the background to the right of the garden was a high whitewashed wall. Two hooded men holding AK-47s flanked three wrought-iron chairs that were pushed up against that wall, facing the camera.

An older woman in traditional Arabic dress sat without her veil in the middle seat, tied to its arms and legs. She was gagged and looked petrified. A young girl sat to her left, an older boy to her right, each of them lashed to the chair and gagged as well.

Hala glared at me. "You speak of fair!" she screamed. "You let him do this to my mother? My children?"

"I had nothing to do with this," I said, turning to Mahoney. "Stop this, Ned. I won't be part of this."

"I couldn't stop it if I wanted to," the FBI agent replied. "This is not something we condone. It is not something we sought."

"Liar!" Hala screeched. "You can stop this."

Mahoney shook his head. "No more than al-Qaeda could stop its people from chopping off the head of that *Wall Street Journal* reporter. I have reason to believe these are Saudi secret policemen. The only people *they* take orders from are much higher up the food chain, men with mindboggling power."

"In the hall, now, or you can forget my involvement," I said; I stood and went out the door.

Mahoney followed me.

"Are those children going to be tortured?" I asked.

"I don't know," my old friend said. "It's out of my hands."

"You asked for this!" I shouted. "You said you were going to wake somebody up, for God's sake!"

"Turns out, most of them were *already* up," Mahoney shot back. "They were contacted by the Saudi government right about the time the good doctor was entering

Union Station. The Saudis intercepted an encrypted e-mail from two high-ranking members of the Family earlier today. So far they've been able to decipher only three words in the whole thing: *Dossari, train,* and *gas.*"

93

"*GAS* LIKE 'CAR GAS' OR *GAS* LIKE 'NERVE GAS'?"

"That's exactly what I'm about to find out, Alex," Mahoney said coldly. "It's why the Saudis offered to create the little telecast in there."

"Ned, you still can't condone the torture—"

"If the Family is plotting some kind of gas attack in the United States, I will do everything in my power to prevent it," Mahoney said sharply. "Does that include accepting help from a regime that does not give its citizens the same rights we have? Yes. I'll live with that if I can save even one American life. Now, you can come back in and help me so this goes only so far, or you can walk away and risk being partly responsible for the deaths of hundreds, maybe thousands of people."

"That's bullshit and unfair," I said.

"In situations like these, life is bullshit and unfair!"

Mahoney shouted, and then he lowered his voice. "I need you, Alex. I need you to help me crack her so we can stop whatever she's got planned."

I shook my head. There was no right answer here; neither position was nobler than the other. Was I going to side with torture or with mass murder on the day after my dear Savior's birth?

Before I could decide, we heard a scream from the interrogation room. Mahoney spun from me and went back in. I hesitated as I heard Hala scream, "No, please!"

I entered the room feeling like a zombie, tired beyond reason and fearing that my soul might be permanently tarnished before the night was over. That sense was intensified when I saw what was happening on the screen.

The hooded men had left Hala's mother where she was, gagged and tied to the chair against the wall. But they had brought the children's chairs close to the table, where they were looking wild-eyed at the camera.

The secret policemen stood behind the children. One carried what looked like a heavy-duty marine battery hitched to jumper cables. The end of the black negative clamp was already attached to the metal chair Hala's son was sitting in. The second guy held the red clamp above it.

Hala looked at me, enraged. "You cannot do this! He's a boy!"

"There were plenty of boys here in DC when you tried to poison the water supply," I said. "But this doesn't have to happen, Doctor. You tell us about the gas attack, and we let your kids and mom go on with their life without you."

"I don't know what you're talking—"

The hooded man barely grazed the back of her son's metal chair with the clamp. The boy's entire body jerked hard and he began to scream and cry.

"Fahd!" Hala cried. "Be brave!"

The boy seemed to hear her, but that only upset him more. He began to squirm and make noises like an animal with a broken leg. One of the men released the boy's gag, and he began to scream in Arabic.

The translator said: "'Mama! Mama, why are they doing this to me?'"

CHAPTER

94

MY STOMACH SOURED AND TURNED. ALL SENSE OF ORDER IN MY BRAIN HAD become disrupted. I thought of my son Ali in that situation and wanted to puke.

I waited for Hala to break. A sob. A tear. Anything. She turned away and looked at the wall, her jaw set.

Mahoney reached over, hit the mute button on the computer, and said, "This can end right now if you tell us about the gas."

She said nothing.

"Turn the camera on us," I said. "Let Fahd see us and her."

Mahoney tapped a couple of buttons, and a small image of the interrogation room appeared in one corner of the screen. "Fahd?" I said. "Can you hear me? Can you see your mother?"

Hala was trying not to glance at the screen. The boy's

hysterics had slowed, but when he saw his mother, they began again. "They are everywhere in the house." He sobbed. "Men and women everywhere. In the washrooms and the pantry and the servants' quarters."

Hala spoke coldly to him. "That is why I have always taught the two of you that the most important thing in life is bravery."

"Listen, Fahd," I said. "Sometimes bravery has nothing to do with guns or pain or bullets. Sometimes bravery is just doing the right thing. And at this moment, the right thing would be to help us, so we can help you. Please ask your mother to tell us what we need to know so we can keep everyone safe, and then those people there can go home."

I turned my head toward Hala, who looked at me with utter hatred. One of the men released the gag on her daughter. They'd moved behind her with the battery and cables.

"Tell them what they want, Mama," Fahd said. "Tell them, or they're going to hurt Aamina."

The girl began to squirm, trying to look back over her shoulder to see what the men were doing. They had the black clamp already affixed behind her. The red clamp was inches from joining it.

"I cannot tell them my secrets…because they are evil men," Hala said to her son.

"Mama, please help, please!" Aamina cried.

The hooded man snapped the red clamp to the metal chair, and the girl stiffened and arched toward the camera, straining every muscle in her face, wanting to scream but utterly unable to do it. Her brother was screaming for her, petrified that the men would return to him. I wanted to cry when they took the clamp off the chair, and the girl collapsed into hysterics.

Sweat soaked the armpits of Hala's jail jumpsuit. It had begun to form on her upper lip too. But otherwise she was back to that warrior expression that revealed nothing.

"Mom?" Fahd said. He hiccupped. "Please help us."

"Help them, Doctor," Mahoney said.

The hooded men moved back behind her son, who began craning his neck around, whimpering, and begging his captors to stop as they clamped the negative line to his chair a second time.

The boy looked back to the camera, lost and bewildered, and blubbered out words in Arabic, the same ones, over and over. If they'd been punches, they'd have been knockouts. The shock in Hala's expression was complete and devastating. She began to shrink in her chair, opening her mouth but unable to speak, as Fahd kept repeating those same words.

In my earbud, the translator interpreted. "'Mommy? Why don't you love us?'"

95

HALA'S CHEEK QUIVERED AS IF SHE'D BEEN SLASHED THERE. THEN HER composure simply crumpled and slid away, like dirt down a riverbank.

She began to sob, saying in Arabic, "Mommy does love you! Mommy loves you both more than anything on earth."

"No," her daughter said and started to cry again. "You don't."

"Aamina! Please, you're too young to—"

The hooded man squeezed the red clamp. Fahd screamed, "Mommy, if you love us, please tell them!"

The clamp lowered, almost made contact.

Dr. Al Dossari watched through her tears, trembling, and then she shouted, "Stop! Stop." She looked at me with an expression I'd seen only once in my life, more than thirty years before, in North Carolina—it was on the face of a mother so driven by love that she was able to lift the front end of an old jeep off the back of her ten-year-old daughter.

"I'll tell you," Hala said piteously. "Make them stop."

"A smart choice," Mahoney said softly.

I hung my head and felt ashamed, guilty, disgusted by what I'd been party to. I thought about Henry Fowler, the man I'd coaxed out of murdering his entire family what seemed a lifetime ago, and wondered if this was what he felt when he won those lawsuits. I could see clearly how a man might develop self-hatred by doing the wrong thing to achieve the desired end.

"Dr. Al Dossari," Mahoney said. "When we are finished with our business, I will let you talk with them one last time."

He closed the camera that showed our image but he kept the screen up so she could watch her children being released from their bonds and going to their grandmother.

"Tell us about the gas," I said.

Hala wiped at her eyes. "Nerve gas. It will be used in an attack."

96

OMAR NAZAD COULD NOT REMEMBER EVER HAVING BEEN THIS EXHAUSTED IN HIS entire life. They'd been digging and shoveling for more than an hour and a half in twenty inches of wet snow that had gotten more and more like a massive block of ice as the temperature in DC had plunged and bottomed out at five degrees above zero.

They'd opened a path almost six feet wide and nearly sixty-five yards long.

"I can't go on," Mustapha bitched in Arabic. "I must drink, brother."

"Five yards," Nazad said, gesturing at the short distance that separated them from M Street, which was unplowed but crisscrossed with tracks. "That's all that separates us, brother. Put your back into it and we go on. Quit, and it all has been for nothing."

Saamad was drenched in sweat, but he raised his pick

and began chopping at the remaining snow, breaking off big hunks of it that Nazad and then Mustapha shoveled from the path. After about the third shovelful, it dawned on the Tunisian that there was another way, a better way.

"Stop," he said. "We're done. We'll get the van going like hell and just plow through it."

"What if we get stuck again?" Saamad asked.

"We won't," Nazad said. "I won't allow us to get stuck."

"But what if we do?" Mustapha insisted.

"We'll dig it out!" Nazad yelled, wanting to brain the man with his shovel. "We'll do whatever it takes."

A minute later they were all in the van, back where they'd left it so it would not be seen from the road. The Tunisian debated whether or not to turn on his headlights, opted to go with running lights, just enough to see the way forward.

He stepped gingerly on the gas, heard the dreaded whine of the tires spinning, and then the treads caught and they crept forward, first at a crawl, and then faster.

"Here we go!" Nazad said, cocking his head to see with his good eye.

"Brother! Stop!" Saamad cried, pointing to their left, out onto M Street and the flashing red and yellow lights coming their way.

Nazad slammed on the brakes and shut down the running lights.

Two snowplows struggled down their side of the street, one trailing the other, throwing all the snow in two lanes toward them, leaving a compacted wall of snow and ice six feet high and fifteen feet deep.

97

"TALK, DOCTOR," I SAID. "THOSE MEN ARE STILL WITH AAMINA AND FAHD."

"You must guarantee me that their safety will—" she began.

Mahoney grabbed her chin. "We guarantee you nothing until we hear what you have to say."

She shook her chin free, glared at me.

"Where's the nerve gas?" I demanded. "Where's it going?"

Hala hesitated, glanced at the computer screen and her children with her mother. She said, "It's on a train heading north."

Once Hala began talking, she seemed to enjoy our reactions to an audacious scheme designed to kill thousands and instill panic once again in New York City. She said that men loyal to Al Ayla worked janitorial services at Pinkler Industries, a chemical-manufacturing concern in South Carolina. The Family members discovered that Pinkler had developed a radical new compound belonging to the organophosphate family of chemicals.

"The basis of all modern pesticides and of nerve gases, such as sarin and VX," Mahoney said, sitting forward.

Hala nodded. "The new compound could be processed precisely enough to eliminate a single species of insect in a field while allowing others to live. But it could also be used to create a gas far more deadly than either sarin or VX. We learned there was to be a shipment of the organophosphate, three barrels of it, going to a pesticide-manufacturing facility in New York. We found out it would be on a train heading north on Christmas Eve, that it would pass through Union Station and end up at a freight facility on the west shore of the Hudson River. Someone loyal to our cause would see all of it transferred onto a barge bound for Manhattan."

I frowned, not sure if I bought the story. "Back up a second. What was *your* job?"

"I stopped the train."

I glanced at Mahoney, whose initial confusion gave way to understanding. "All of that was just to stop the train?"

"Yes."

"Where?"

Hala shrugged, said, "Somewhere outside the First Street tunnel before it goes under Capitol Hill and through Union Station to the Ivy City Yard."

I knew exactly where she was talking about. As young teenagers, Sampson and I had climbed the fence and gone into the tunnel a couple of hundred yards before we heard a train coming at us. Wasn't that the fastest I'd ever run?

Mahoney asked, "So, what, you stopped the train long enough for someone to steal the barrels?"

She shook her head a little too quickly and said, "I stopped it long enough for a PhD student in chemistry to attach a timed system that will convert the compound to nerve gas when triggered."

"And?" I asked. "Who is going to trigger it?"

Hala shrugged. "Whoever is in the van that is supposed to meet the freight barge tomorrow afternoon."

"Driver's name?" Mahoney demanded.

"I don't know," she said. "I didn't need to know. It's better that way."

"So the van driver meets the freight barge, and then what?" I asked.

She smiled. "He places the barrels in his van, triggers the system, puts on a gas mask, and drives around the city letting the gas escape, starting with Wall Street right after the markets close."

I flashed on the freight train that I'd seen after Hala was caught, coming from that tunnel and heading toward the Ivy City Yard, and remembered how it had made me think that some semblance of normalcy had returned to Union Station.

Actually, I'd been watching a chemical weapon pass right under everyone's nose.

CHAPTER

98

I CHECKED MY WATCH: 12:31 A.M. CHRISTMAS HAD COME AND GONE, AND SO
had my promise to Bree, along with an innocence that I
had not known I had left to lose. But of course, although
I'd heard testimony about it, had gathered evidence in its
wake, I had never personally seen children tortured before.

The freight train had gotten at least a three-hour head
start. But it was traveling in the wake of a nor'easter bar-
reling toward New York. We'd catch the train, stop it, and
disarm that triggering device.

Mahoney seemed to think the same thing. He got up
and left the room to arrange for the Critical Incident
Response Group to mobilize while he made plans to in-
tercept the train.

I studied Hala, who was staring at the table as if she

couldn't believe she was in this position: a traitor to her cause.

I said, "Which freight car carries those organophosphates?"

Hala looked at me as if she had one last card to play. "Twenty-ninth behind the engine," she said. "It's green with CSX and C. Itoh markings. You can't miss it."

FIFTEEN MINUTES LATER, AT A QUARTER TO ONE IN THE MORNING, I STOOD IN the snow on the roof of the detention center with Ned Mahoney, waiting for a U.S. Marine helicopter that was coming in from Quantico loaded with members of the Critical Incident Response Group.

"We've got a location on the train," Mahoney said. "It's almost to Trenton. We'll stop it somewhere north of there, someplace rural."

"What if it's booby-trapped?" I asked.

"Believe me, we'll be wearing full HAZMAT gear," Mahoney said. "Sounds sporty, doesn't it? I can't believe you don't want to be there to see this through."

I'd known Mahoney for nearly fifteen years, worked side by side with him for several of those years, had been to his home too many times to count, knew all the doings of his wife and children. And yet right then, he seemed a stranger to me.

"I didn't like what went on in that room, Ned," I said.

"You think I did, Alex?" he shot back.

"It's beneath us."

"It is," he agreed, pain rippling through his face. "Shows you that you've got to meet people like that on their own turf, using their rules. It's a sad thing to say, but true."

"They were kids."

"They were leverage against an insane scheme."

I heard the thumping of the helicopter coming, saw the spotlight on its belly. "What if her attorney finds out, Ned? Demands to see a tape of the interrogation. Everything Hala told us will be fruit of the poisoned tree, disallowed in court."

"Not everything has to play out in court," Mahoney replied coldly. "Besides, when I raised my hand there just before we began, the battery pack on the camera in the observation booth mysteriously fell off. Anything that went on beyond that is baseless hearsay on Dr. Al Dossari's part, her word against ours, and who is a judge going to trust, Alex? A twenty-year veteran of the FBI and the legendary Dr. Alex Cross, or a madwoman willing to send nerve gas into Manhattan?"

I gazed at him as if he were transforming before my eyes, seeing new dimensions to his character. "I never pegged you as a master strategist, Ned."

He raised his arm to block the snow being thrown up by the helicopter, yelled, "I have my moments. You can take my car home if you're good to drive."

"I'll make it," I said and accepted the keys as the chopper settled into the snow. "Ned?"

"What's that, Alex?"

"Be careful," I said. "You've got a lot of people to come back to."

Mahoney locked gazes with me, understanding. He shook my hand. "Thanks, Alex. It means a lot."

100

I MADE IT HOME AT TWO IN THE MORNING ON THE DAY AFTER CHRISTMAS. Everyone had gone to sleep, though the lights on the tree still glowed in the front window, a beacon left on for me, I guessed. Where had the holiday gone?

I kicked off my shoes, climbed the stairs, listened at the doors of my children and my grandmother, and felt drowsy at the rhythm of their breathing. Not even Nana's gentle snoring could keep me awake.

I slipped into my room, dropped my pants, and slid into bed, feeling the heat of Bree's body. Her smell was there too, all around me. She rolled over, laid her head on my chest, murmured, "You okay, baby?"

"I'm good now," I said, and closed my eyes, telling myself to compartmentalize, to take refuge in my own bed with my wife holding me, and rest.

But as I hugged Bree, my mind slipped back and forth

between images of the Al Dossari children under torture and the details of the story Hala told us.

Just before I plunged into sleep, I remembered something I'd said to Mahoney the evening before: *Confessions made under torture can't be taken seriously. They're half-truths mixed with what the tortured person thinks the torturer wants to hear.*

101

FOR AN HOUR AND A HALF, I SLEPT WITH NO DREAMS OF ANYTHING. BUT THEN, from the inky depths of my brain, images began to roll. I saw Hala lobbing the grenade at me. I saw Henry Fowler holding a gun to his ex-wife's head and kicking at his children, who became Hala's kids strapped to the torture chairs.

The Saudi secret policemen in their hoods were there as well, one carrying the battery, the other holding the ends of the jumper cables. The one with the battery pulled off his hood, revealing himself as Mahoney. The second hooded man tried to get away, but Mahoney grinned grimly and tore the hood off his head.

It was me. I was the one who held the jumper-cable clamps. Mahoney and I were laughing, enjoying ourselves the way we'd done dozens of times at backyard barbecues and other family get-togethers.

My dream self opened the red clamp's jaw wide, looked at the children, and seemed fascinated by the terror they displayed. I clamped the cable to Aamina's chair, expecting the arch and trembling I'd seen her exhibit during her torture before.

Instead, I heard a rhythmic buzzing noise that broke the spell and roused me from sleep. I was drenched with sweat. Bree rolled over and slept on. I looked at the clock groggily: 3:40 a.m. I needed at least ten, fourteen more hours, but my bladder felt full. And what was the noise that woke me?

I slid out of bed as carefully as I could, stood, felt wobbly, and then noticed the message light blinking on my mobile. I picked it up, staggered to the bathroom, and sat down on the toilet because I did not think standing was such a good idea. Before I could check the message, the phone began buzzing in my hand, the sound that had wrenched me from sleep.

It was Mahoney.

I accepted the call, peed, and grumbled, "You a vampire or something? Never need sleep."

"Yeah, I'm a new character in that Twilight series my kid's always reading," he replied, and I could hear wind blowing hard.

"Get the nerve gas?"

"We got in a firefight with one of Hala's coconspirators," Mahoney said. "He'd been holding engineers at gunpoint. Sniper got him, and we freed the rail workers. One had been mutilated, his eyeball boiled."

That got me more awake. "What? An engineer's eye?"

"In revenge, because the engineer had done the same thing to the dead guy's partner, with hot coffee. It's a long story for another time. But they, the engineers, said the partner left the train in the First Street tunnel and went back toward the entrance, where the third man in the rail crew, a Robby Simon, had disappeared."

"You find the organophosphates and the triggering device in car twenty-nine?"

"There were three blue barrels with Pinkler Industries labels in car twenty-nine," Mahoney replied. "But when we opened them, we found sand and gravel."

I remembered the enthusiasm Hala had shown when she'd described the plot.

"She fed us half-truths mixed with what we wanted to hear," I said, furious at myself for wanting to believe her confession so much that I'd set aside my suspicions.

"My instincts were right," Mahoney said. "She stopped the train so other Al Ayla members could steal the chemicals."

My hand shot to my temple. "And they're here. In DC."

"Last known whereabouts: two miles from Congress."

"Jesus Christ," I said.

"We're going back to Hala," Mahoney said.

I flashed with dread on the image of her kids being tortured.

"You're going, Ned," I said. "I'm done with that."

I ended the call and shut the ringer off. I intended to return to bed. But then I realized that I was no more than fifteen blocks from where Hala's accomplices had stolen the organophosphates.

So was my family.

My first reaction was to wake them all, move them from the area until the three barrels were found and neutralized.

But then old habits reasserted themselves. *Snow on the ground,* I thought. They had to have left evidence around there somewhere.

I picked up the phone and called the man I trusted more than anyone in my life.

CHAPTER

102

OMAR NAZAD SAT IN THE CAB OF THE VAN, FEELING HIS STINGING HANDS AND feet begin to thaw, and stared through the windshield at the one hundred and twenty cubic yards of snow and ice that still lay between him and M Street.

He and the Algerians had broken up and removed at least that amount in the past three hours. They were still only halfway to the road. They hadn't eaten in twelve hours. And they hadn't had anything to drink for six. The snow they put in their mouths seemed to make them even thirstier.

"Inshallah," the Tunisian kept muttering to himself. *The will of Allah. It is God's will that we must suffer and sacrifice and suffer again in order to defeat His enemies. This is a gift, somehow. A blessing.*

"We should leave, brother," Mustapha said from the passenger seat.

"I agree," Saamad said. "Leave while we still can."

Nazad looked at them like they were mad. "Leave the best weapon the Family's ever had? No. That is not what God wants."

"But what if Allah wants us to get caught and sent to prison?" Saamad demanded.

"Shut up," Nazad said. He was sick of the Algerians, how quick they were to cut and run. It had to be the French influence.

"I have to eat something, drink something," Mustapha complained.

"I can't help you."

"Maybe there was food in that shed," Saamad said. "Water too."

Nazad looked at him again. "You didn't search the entire place?"

Mustapha shrugged. "The shovels and picks were right by the door."

Moments later they were all following the path the Algerians had taken to the toolshed earlier. The door hung open on its hinges, flapped in the wind. They went inside, flashed their lights, and saw a portable generator, half a dozen power tools, a jackhammer, three sledgehammers, more picks, a row of hard hats, a surveyor's transom, and a cooler. Mustapha and Saamad went straight to the cooler, yanked it open, and cried out in delight.

Saamad grabbed a granola bar and a frozen bottle of Gatorade, shook them at Nazad. "Allah be praised! Food and drink, brother."

"And a jackhammer!" Mustapha cried.

But the Tunisian paid them no mind. He was staring at a metal box attached to the wall and sealed with a Master Lock. On instinct, he retrieved one of the sledgehammers and tried to break the lock, but he couldn't. He looked closely at the other tools now at his disposal and smiled.

Nazad started the generator. Then he plugged in a Benner-Nawman rebar cutter. He fit the hasp of the lock into the jaws of the cutter and flipped it on. The jaws bit and snapped it in less than a second.

The Algerians had been gnawing on frozen granola bars while he worked. Only when Nazad set the cutter down and pulled open the door to the box did Mustapha become interested.

"What do you find in there, brother?" he asked.

The Tunisian was beaming already, feeling blessed once again by God. The first thing his headlamp had revealed in the box was a row of keys hanging on hooks, all neat and orderly and tagged.

The first key on the right said CAT D6K.

103

"YOU WOKE ME OUT OF A PERFECTLY GOOD SLEEP TO RIDE IN A SARDINE CAN?"
John Sampson groaned, trying to get his massive frame
into Mahoney's Subaru at around four in the morning. He
wore a snorkel jacket, hood up, and peered at me blearily
from inside the fur trim. He took the travel cup of coffee
I offered him.

"Need help checking out a potential crime scene before
I call in an evidence team," I said, putting the Forester in
gear. All-wheel drive and weighed down with Sampson's
and my combined four hundred and thirty pounds, the
car moved like a mini tank into the tracks other cars had
made going up and down Sampson's street.

"Potential crime scene?" Sampson asked, annoyed.

"I don't know exactly where the crime scene is, John,"
I explained. "That's why I need you. To help find it."

He groaned, drank the coffee. "Why do I feel like I'm two hundred moves behind you, Alex?"

"Because in this case you are," I said, and I filled him in, finishing with the information that members of Al Ayla had likely pulled nerve-gas components off a freight train stopped near the entrance to the tunnel system.

"I know where that is." Sampson grunted. "Remember running out of there when we were kids?"

"Probably the only time I've ever beaten you in a race," I said.

"Found a body in the right-of-way there six or seven years ago."

I'd forgotten, but now I nodded and said, "Emily Rodriguez."

"Poor little thing," Sampson said. "What was she, seven? Son of a bitch tortured her something awful before he killed her."

I flashed on Hala's daughter, also seven, arching against the electric current, and said, "But what do you think? Freeway side of the tracks, or M Street?"

"Freeway," Sampson said. "M Street, you're gonna need boots. It's a good walk to the tracks and they've got construction going there on that off-ramp they've been building forever."

"But the freeway side is super-steep going down to the tracks," I reminded him. "Fifty-five-gallon drum weighs a lot, and being up on the freeway is just too visible, even in a blizzard. I'm thinking they went in on the M Street side, big walk or not."

"Hell, what do I know?" Sampson said. "I'm just along for the ride."

The snowbanks along Eleventh Street were as high as I'd ever seen them, like in pictures of Anchorage or Nome. Sampson and I had to strain to spot the security fence where Eleventh Street crossed over the tunnel's mouth.

I parked right in the middle of the street above the tunnel, threw on the hazard lights, told Sampson to move the car if someone came along. Before he could grumble about that, I got out, went to the snowbank, and crawled up it to the fence.

I got out my Maglite, shone it down through the chain links, and immediately saw footprints on both sides of the track where it entered the tunnel. Farther back on the bank facing M Street, the snow had been pounded down, leaving a path five or six feet wide.

I snatched up my cell phone, called Metro dispatch, and requested an evidence wagon and full team to join me at the corner of Eleventh and M Streets. Lucy, the dispatcher, a friend of mine, said it might be an hour before they could get the team there, what with all the snow.

"John Sampson and I will secure the scene and wait for them," I said. "Thanks, Lucy."

Snapping shut my mobile, I sat down on the snowbank and edged out, then started sliding. I hit the pavement, landed upright, and was walking back to the idling Subaru, cleaning the snow off the seat of my pants, when I heard a heavy engine backfire and then rumble to life southeast of me, toward M Street.

104

PRAISE ALLAH!

When the bulldozer had fired up after he'd found a can of ether under the seat and sprayed it into the fuel tank, Omar Nazad wanted to weep. Instead, he thanked God over and over for blessing him, eased off on the choke until the engine ran smooth, and studied the diagram of the control levers until he thought he understood them.

The Tunisian looked overhead, saw a toggle switch, and flipped it. Small spotlights on top of the bulldozer cab lit up the area directly in front of him. He pulled a lever back, and the blade came under his control, groaned, and rose. The Algerians, who'd been standing off to the side, began to cheer and shake their fists.

Feeling possessed now, Nazad studied the diagram once more and threw a second lever forward. He felt something engage. He pressed the throttle. The bulldozer bucked, broke free of the ice holding its treads, and began to grind forward through the snow, past the van and toward the hundred and twenty cubic yards of frozenness that separated them from M Street and escape.

"Saamad, get in the van!" Nazad shouted. "Mustapha, get up on the bank where you can see the road, make sure I'm aiming in the right direction."

Saamad nodded and ran to the van. Mustapha seemed annoyed at the request Nazad had made of him, but he trotted along in front of the bulldozer blade, toward the wall of snow and the road.

Nazad slowed just shy of the huge snowbank, dropped the blade, and set the transmission in a lower gear. He watched Mustapha climb the snowbank. Then he saw headlights swing off Eleventh Street into the eastbound lanes of M Street.

Until that moment, the Tunisian had been nearly pathological about avoiding attention. He'd kept the van well back from the road, and as they'd dug through the night, every time a vehicle had approached, he'd ordered his men to dive down onto their bellies and wait until the headlights passed.

Now he did not care, especially when the Algerian informed him that the approaching car was a little white Subaru Forester, a commuter vehicle, certainly no police squad car. Nazad pressed down the throttle again after the Forester went by, focused on the blade as it struck the snowbank. It bit and pushed, and then the entire front end of the bulldozer began to climb, pushing snow ahead of it.

Here we go, the Tunisian thought. *There is nothing that can stop us now.*

105

"**WHAT THE HELL IS THAT DOING HERE?**" **I SHOUTED AT SAMPSON, LOOKING** over my shoulder as I tried to get a better view of the bulldozer that had surged up on top of the snowbank and was pushing snow out onto M Street.

As the bulldozer backed down the other side of the snowbank, Sampson said, "Construction company that's building the off-ramp probably sent him out to clear the site before the rest of the crew arrives."

"At four fifteen in the morning on the day after Christmas?"

"Didn't you read that piece in the *Post* last week? They're getting all sorts of heat on this thing. People say that ramp is way over budget and should have been done two years ago."

"Well, we've got to get him to stop," I said, driving

into the traffic rotary by the Washington Yacht Club and heading back.

I pulled over and parked well away from the bulldozer, hazard lights blinking. Sampson and I got out just as the bulldozer crested the bank a second time, pushing more snow out across M Street and completely blocking the westbound lanes. Then it backed down until we could barely see the top of it.

The bulldozer's spotlight beams lit up a guy standing on top of the snowbank who was dressed in a blue work jumpsuit of some kind. He seemed to be directing the machine operator and did not notice us coming down the street toward him. We plodded up to him through the rubble field the bulldozer was creating, punching through snow up to our shins.

I waved my hands at him, shouted, "Hey! Tell the driver to stop!"

The man stiffened, took a few steps toward us, put his hand to his ear. "What?"

"Shut off that bulldozer!" Sampson yelled, and he shone a flashlight on the badge he was holding. "Metro DC Police!"

The bulldozer surged up again. The man froze, and then nodded. He ran toward the cab. I couldn't make out any details of the driver.

"Police!" the man yelled. "They said stop!"

The machine ground to a halt atop the snowbank. The engine dropped into an idle.

"What is the matter?" the man on the snowbank called.

"Sir, could you come down here?" I called back. "We believe this is a crime scene. Who told you to clear the construction site?"

The man hesitated, tapped his ear as if to indicate he could not hear me with the dozer so close, and then crouched as if he were going to butt-slide down the snowbank to me. I heard the whine of hydraulic lines engaging and glanced up and over at the bulldozer blade starting to rise.

"CSX?" Sampson said.

Sampson trained his Maglite on the chest of the guy sitting on top of the snowbank. The patch on the jacket said CSX. Why would train workers be clearing out a federal construction site at four fifteen in the morning?

I started reaching casually for my service pistol, wishing that I was not standing in deep snow, and readjusted the beam of my own flashlight until it shone up and through the windshield of the bulldozer. Just before the blade got high enough to block my view, I saw a man wearing a blue CSX coat. His right eye was covered in bandages.

CHAPTER

106

"GUN!" SAMPSON ROARED. HE LEAPED TO HIS RIGHT AND GOT DOWN INTO A combat shooting crouch, clawing for his weapon.

My Glock came free of its holster and I saw the man lying prone on the snowbank just before he shot. The round hit low in front of me and sprayed chips of ice everywhere.

Up to our knees in that chunky snow, vulnerable due to the high ground, Sampson and I were the proverbial fish in the barrel. But Sampson didn't seem to feel that way. He squeezed off two shots at the gunman on the snowbank just as the bulldozer engine roared. Both rounds hit left of the prone man, and he immediately returned fire. I was aiming the Glock when I heard the crack of his bullet passing an inch from my head. My shot hit beneath him.

The bulldozer clanked into gear and came straight

down the snowbank at us, blade up, blocking any shot at the windshield.

Both Sampson and I are tall. I'm six two. He's got three inches on me. Which means we have long legs, which we used to run in opposite directions. Sampson went straight at the one shooting at us, firing nonstop, driving back the man on the snowbank.

I tripped and sprawled in the last deep snow before the plowed road. My shoulder smashed hard against an ice boulder, and I felt bones break and things tear apart.

The pain of the impact and the shock that blew through my system were indescribable. Eyes closed, gritting my teeth, I moaned and felt my pistol fall from a hand that no longer worked.

"Alex!" Sampson yelled above the roar of the bulldozer.

I forced open my eyes, peered through the spots that danced there. Sampson was sixty feet from me, less than ten feet from the bulldozer blade, scrambling toward the plowed road to Eleventh Street.

He slipped, stumbled. The blade closed the gap.

"John!" I croaked, trying to get to my feet, realizing that my entire right arm was useless and dangling at my side.

My oldest friend had been a great athlete in his day, a man with deceptively fluid moves and an uncanny sense of balance. But Sampson was DC through and through, not used to running in snow. When the blade was less than three feet from him, he stumbled again, and I thought he was about to take the hit of his life right there on M Street.

CHAPTER

107

THE GUY UP ON THE SNOWBANK SHOT AT SAMPSON WHEN LESS THAN A FOOT
separated Sampson from the bulldozer blade. The bullet
hit the upper back part of the blade, ricocheted, and shattered the bulldozer's windshield.

The machine lurched hard left, as if the driver had
ducked and pulled the steering wheel. Now the blade was
coming right at me from about fifty feet away. I got to one
knee and then up to my feet, gasping at the pain shooting
everywhere around my right shoulder.

Gun.

The butt of my Glock was right there in the snow,
the barrel buried all the way to the trigger. I grabbed
at it with my left hand and pulled it from the snow as
the bulldozer closed on me. I heard someone shoot, and
someone scream.

I stood unsteadily, my right arm swinging stupidly at

my side. But my survival voices were taking over: *Wait until he's right there, and then jump to the side, just off the blade. Clear the steel treads, and you'll have your shot at him. Left-handed, but you should be close enough.*

But then a louder voice screamed, *Snow! You've got snow in your barrel. Pull the trigger, and your barrel explodes!*

The bulldozer was right on me then, no more than ten feet away, and I was sure my entire body was about to feel like my right shoulder. But then it dawned on me that the driver could no longer see me, that the blade was blocking him, that he was driving blind.

I jumped. The upper corner of the blade just missed my head. I landed, jumped again, pivoted, hoping to aim the gun at the driver and tell him I'd shoot if—

Sampson's gun went off behind me. I heard the bullet ping inside the cab. The driver did what I absolutely did not expect. He jumped out of the cab, landing awkwardly in the snow about three feet away, while the bulldozer kept on, climbing the snowbank on the median strip, headed toward an office building across the street.

I raised my gun at the one-eyed man even as he raised his gun at me.

108

OUR WEAPONS WERE LESS THAN TWO INCHES APART. THE ONE-EYED TERRORIST and I were in a Mexican standoff that looked like a no-winner for me any way it went down. If he pulled the trigger, I was dead. If I pulled the trigger, my barrel would explode and I was dead. Maybe he was dead too, but I was definitely in a black body bag with a grieving wife and family.

The man's uncovered eye was wide and glistening. "In-shallah!" he whispered to me.

I got it. We were both in the hands of God now, about to discover His will.

The sound of the bulldozer crashing into something was followed by a gunshot that came from behind and above me. Both the driver and I instinctively cringed and ducked, but I recovered much quicker.

My arms were longer than his. I probably had three,

four inches of reach on him. My right arm was useless, but my left had been bent as I aimed my plugged gun at him, not extended at all.

My left hand jabbed at him, setting him up for a straight impossible-to-deliver right cross. Instead, I slapped the side of his pistol hard to his left with the barrel of my gun and then stepped into his very, very large blind spot.

The terrorist shot wildly. Sampson fired at virtually the same time, and I heard the sound of a hit and the cry of a wounded man somewhere up on the snowbank before I chopped down with my pistol, hitting the man right in the bandages, right on the bone above the socket of his scalded eye.

His knees left him, and so did everything else. He crashed onto his side, out cold.

109

A WEEK LATER, IT WAS RAINING AND WARM; THE DEEP FREEZE THAT HAD gripped the city so severely was gone, and the snow had turned into slush and puddles. But that would not stop me from taking my wife out for dinner and dancing on New Year's Eve. We were going to double-date with John Sampson and his wife, Billie. We'd done it up right, rented a car and driver to chauffeur us to our dinner at the rooftop-terrace restaurant of the W Hotel—best view in the city—and then across the river to the Havana Breeze Latin Club in Fairfax for a little salsa, a little merengue.

Why not? We were all in a mood to celebrate, and a jazz club just wasn't going to do it. After all, we'd not only put Hala Al Dossari and her coconspirators in prison, we'd also foiled their ultimate plot, which was a doozy.

Documents that we'd discovered in the terrorists' van

laid out the plan: The stolen chemicals were to be held for twenty-six days in a basement apartment Nazad had rented on Capitol Hill. Early on the morning of January 20, Nazad, a trained chemist, would mix the organophosphates in a rented five-hundred-gallon water tank. Then he and his accomplices would put the tank full of the crude nerve-gas agent in the back of a pickup truck and skirt the closed roads in the city until they got upwind of the Capitol.

Then they would all don masks, do the final mix, and spray the chemicals up into the prevailing winds, in the hope that the toxic vapor cloud would drift over the massive crowds gathered on the National Mall and across to the back steps of the Capitol, where the chief justice of the U.S. Supreme Court would be swearing in the president of the United States.

It was so crazy, it might have worked. Hundreds, maybe thousands might have died. The president might have died, and the justices, and every member of Congress. It was so crazy, I didn't want to think about it anymore, I decided at around six that New Year's Eve as I waited in the kitchen for Bree to finish with her hair and finally choose the dress she was going to wear for our big night out on the town.

My younger son, Ali, and Jannie and Ava were devouring a plate of fried rabbit, one of my grandmother's specialties. Ava had balked at the idea at first, but once she saw Jannie and Ali tearing into it, she'd tried it, and now she was on her second piece.

"Good, huh?" I asked.

"Better than good," Ava said. "I had no idea rabbit could taste this amazing. Like chicken, but way, way better."

"It's the buttermilk," Nana Mama said, looking pleased as she scrubbed out the cast-iron skillet she'd used to fry the rabbit. "I soak the meat in buttermilk overnight to make it tender like that."

"Damon's gonna be mad when he hears you made fried rabbit *after* he went back to school," Jannie remarked.

"Damon could have stayed home until tomorrow," my grandmother responded. "He chose to go back early."

"To get ahead on his studies," I reminded her.

"Can't fault him for that," Nana Mama allowed. "But even the best choices sometimes have adverse consequences."

"Like missing fried rabbit," Ali said.

Nana smiled and pointed at her great-grandson. "See there? Always said you were a smart, smart boy."

Ali grinned from ear to ear and reached for the last piece of rabbit, but Ava got to it first. He groaned.

"I'll split it with you," Ava said.

My grandmother squinted in my direction. "How you doing?"

"Twenty-four hours since my last pain pill and it doesn't bark at me unless I move it," I said, glancing down at my right arm, which was in a sling.

I'd broken my clavicle, dislocated my shoulder, and cracked the head of my humerus bone falling as I tried to get out of the way of the bulldozer. A surgeon had put me back together four days ago. In three months, he'd said, I'd be good as new.

Bree came into the kitchen wearing a very flattering black cocktail dress and a pair of black stiletto heels.

Nana Mama whistled at her. So did I.

"You really going to go out with Alex looking like that?" my grandmother asked in a playful tone.

Bree's face fell. "What's wrong with it?"

"There's nothing wrong with that outfit," Nana Mama replied. "Everything's right with that outfit. But look at the man who's going with you to ring in the New Year. Arm in a sling, looking all beat-up. People'll think you got to be his nurse. That's not the kind of man you want holding your hand when you're dressed like you're in a movie or something."

Everyone was laughing, including me.

Bree threw her arms around my neck, kissed me on the cheek, and said, "Honey, from where I'm standing, you're looking fine."

"Even with a busted shoulder?" I said.

"You wear it well," she assured me, and she kissed me again before looking at my grandmother. "Am I right?"

Nana Mama tried to look skeptical, but then she cracked up.

The doorbell rang. The driver had come for us. Nana Mama and the kids watched us through the front window as we were driven away. Dinner was off-the-charts great. So was the Chilean wine Sampson ordered.

We got to the Havana Breeze around ten thirty, took a booth, and ordered mojitos. Billie told Sampson she wanted to dance right away.

"Who can argue with that?" he replied.

They went out on the dance floor. I was nursing my drink and having a good old time watching my towering best friend try to samba with Billie, who even in high heels barely reached his chest.

"You're something, I ever tell you that, Alex?" Bree asked.

I glanced over at my wife, who looked dazzling.

"What nonsense are you talking now, woman?" I asked.

Bree smiled, shook her head, said, "No, seriously. I don't know how you do it, but despite all the chaos you get yourself into and out of, you find a way to keep your balance. I love the fact that even though you're called into these horrible situations where you see the worst in people, you somehow manage to remain a fundamentally good person."

I flashed on the hooded men behind Hala Al Dossari's children. I felt my expression darken, and I looked away from her, saying, "I don't know about that sometimes."

She took my chin, turned my face back to her. "Listen to me. You, Alex Cross, are the best man I know."

I looked into her eyes, hating the fact that I had to keep things from her, hating the fact that I had already secretly met with Father Harris twice so I could try to make sense of what Ned and I had done to prevent a nerve-gas attack on Inauguration Day.

I kissed Bree, said, "And you're the best woman I've ever known."

A hip-moving salsa tune came over the speakers.

"So let's dance," I said.

"You want me to dance with a man in a sling?" Bree asked.

"Uh, you said I wore it well."

"Did I say that?" she asked, watching me.

"You did," I said. I slid from the booth and held out my good hand for her.

My wife took it, smiled, and got up. But she hesitated at moving to the dance floor, leaned into me, and said over the pulsing music: "Alex, are you all right?"

"I have the sexiest, most beautiful woman in the club with me," I replied. "It's almost twelve. And we're about to ring in the New Year in each other's arms. How could I not be all right?"

ABOUT THE AUTHOR

JAMES PATTERSON has created more enduring fictional characters than any other novelist writing today. He is the author of the Alex Cross novels, the most popular detective series of the past twenty-five years, including *Kiss the Girls* and *Along Came a Spider*. Mr. Patterson also writes the bestselling Women's Murder Club novels, set in San Francisco, and the top-selling New York detective series of all time, featuring Detective Michael Bennett. James Patterson has had more *New York Times* bestsellers than any other writer, ever, according to *Guinness World Records*. Since his first novel won the Edgar Award in 1977, James Patterson's books have sold more than 300 million copies.

James Patterson has also written numerous #1 bestsellers for young readers, including the Maximum Ride, Witch & Wizard, and Middle School series. In total, these books have spent more than 330 weeks on national bestseller lists. In 2010, James Patterson was named Author of the Year at the Children's Choice Book Awards.

His lifelong passion for books and reading led James Patterson to create the innovative website ReadKiddoRead.com, giving adults an invaluable tool to find the books that get kids reading for life. He writes full-time and lives in Florida with his family.

BOOKS BY JAMES PATTERSON

FEATURING ALEX CROSS

Cross Justice

Hope to Die

Cross My Heart

Alex Cross, Run

Merry Christmas, Alex Cross

Kill Alex Cross

Cross Fire

I, Alex Cross

Alex Cross's Trial (with Richard DiLallo)

Cross Country

Double Cross

Cross (also published as *Alex Cross*)

Mary, Mary

London Bridges

The Big Bad Wolf

Four Blind Mice

Violets Are Blue

Roses Are Red

Pop Goes the Weasel

Cat & Mouse

Jack & Jill

Kiss the Girls

Along Came a Spider

THE WOMEN'S MURDER CLUB

14th Deadly Sin (with Maxine Paetro)

Unlucky 13 (with Maxine Paetro)

12th of Never (with Maxine Paetro)

11th Hour (with Maxine Paetro)

10th Anniversary (with Maxine Paetro)

The 9th Judgment (with Maxine Paetro)

The 8th Confession (with Maxine Paetro)

7th Heaven (with Maxine Paetro)

The 6th Target (with Maxine Paetro)

The 5th Horseman (with Maxine Paetro)

4th of July (with Maxine Paetro)

3rd Degree (with Andrew Gross)

2nd Chance (with Andrew Gross)

1st to Die

FEATURING MICHAEL BENNETT

Alert (with Michael Ledwidge)

Burn (with Michael Ledwidge)

Gone (with Michael Ledwidge)

I, Michael Bennett (with Michael Ledwidge)

Tick Tock (with Michael Ledwidge)

Worst Case (with Michael Ledwidge)

Run for Your Life (with Michael Ledwidge)

Step on a Crack (with Michael Ledwidge)

THE PRIVATE NOVELS

Private Vegas (with Maxine Paetro)
Private India: City on Fire (with Ashwin Sanghi)
Private Down Under (with Michael White)
Private L.A. (with Mark Sullivan)
Private Berlin (with Mark Sullivan)
Private London (with Mark Pearson)
Private Games (with Mark Sullivan)
Private: #1 Suspect (with Maxine Paetro)
Private (with Maxine Paetro)

THE NYPD RED NOVELS

NYPD Red 3 (with Marshall Karp)
NYPD Red 2 (with Marshall Karp)
NYPD Red (with Marshall Karp)

STANDALONE BOOKS

The Murder House (with David Ellis)
Truth or Die (with Howard Roughan)
Miracle at Augusta (with Peter de Jonge)
Invisible (with David Ellis)
Mistress (with David Ellis)
Second Honeymoon (with Howard Roughan)
Zoo (with Michael Ledwidge)
Guilty Wives (with David Ellis)
The Christmas Wedding (with Richard DiLallo)
Kill Me If You Can (with Marshall Karp)
Now You See Her (with Michael Ledwidge)
Toys (with Neil McMahon)
Don't Blink (with Howard Roughan)
The Postcard Killers (with Liza Marklund)
The Murder of King Tut (with Martin Dugard)
Swimsuit (with Maxine Paetro)
Against Medical Advice (with Hal Friedman)
Sail (with Howard Roughan)
Sundays at Tiffany's (with Gabrielle Charbonnet)
You've Been Warned (with Howard Roughan)
The Quickie (with Michael Ledwidge)
Judge & Jury (with Andrew Gross)
Beach Road (with Peter de Jonge)
Lifeguard (with Andrew Gross)
Honeymoon (with Howard Roughan)

Sam's Letters to Jennifer
The Lake House
The Jester (with Andrew Gross)
The Beach House (with Peter de Jonge)
Suzanne's Diary for Nicholas
Cradle and All
When the Wind Blows
Miracle on the 17th Green (with Peter de Jonge)
Hide & Seek
The Midnight Club
Black Friday (originally published as *Black Market*)
See How They Run (originally published as *The Jericho Commandment*)
Season of the Machete
The Thomas Berryman Number

FOR ADULTS AND TEENS

Confessions: The Murder of an Angel (with Maxine Paetro)
Maximum Ride Forever
Witch & Wizard: The Lost (with Emily Raymond)
Confessions: The Paris Mysteries (with Maxine Paetro)
Homeroom Diaries (with Lisa Papademetriou, illustrated by Keino)
First Love (with Emily Raymond)
Confessions: The Private School Murders (with Maxine Paetro)
Witch & Wizard: The Kiss (with Jill Dembowski)
Confessions of a Murder Suspect (with Maxine Paetro)
Nevermore: A Maximum Ride Novel
Witch & Wizard: The Fire (with Jill Dembowski)
Angel: A Maximum Ride Novel
Witch & Wizard: The Gift (with Ned Rust)
Med Head (with Hal Friedman)
FANG: A Maximum Ride Novel
Witch & Wizard (with Gabrielle Charbonnet)
MAX: A Maximum Ride Novel
The Final Warning: A Maximum Ride Novel
Saving the World and Other Extreme Sports: A Maximum Ride Novel
School's Out—Forever: A Maximum Ride Novel
Maximum Ride: The Angel Experiment

FOR YOUNGER READERS

House of Robots: Robots Go Wild (with Chris Grabenstein, illustrated by Juliana Neufeld)
Treasure Hunters: Secret of the Forbidden City (with Chris Grabenstein, illustrated by Juliana Neufeld)

Daniel X: Lights Out (with Chris Grabenstein)

Middle School, Just My Rotten Luck (with Chris Tebbetts, illustrated by Laura Park)

Public School Superhero (with Chris Tebbetts, illustrated by Cory Thomas)

I Totally Funniest (with Chris Grabenstein, illustrated by Laura Park)

House of Robots (with Chris Grabenstein, illustrated by Juliana Neufeld)

Treasure Hunters: Danger Down the Nile (with Chris Grabenstein, illustrated by Juliana Neufeld)

Middle School, Save Rafe! (with Chris Tebbetts, illustrated by Laura Park)

Middle School, Ultimate Showdown (with Julia Bergen, illustrated by Alec Longstreth)

I Even Funnier (with Chris Grabenstein, illustrated by Laura Park)

Treasure Hunters (with Chris Grabenstein and Mark Shulman, illustrated by Juliana Neufeld)

Middle School, How I Survived Bullies, Broccoli, and Snake Hill (with Chris Tebbetts, illustrated by Laura Park)

Middle School, My Brother Is a Big, Fat Liar (with Lisa Papademetriou, illustrated by Neil Swaab)

I Funny (with Chris Grabenstein)

Daniel X: Armageddon (with Chris Grabenstein)

Middle School, Get Me out of Here! (with Chris Tebbetts, illustrated by Laura Park)

Daniel X: Game Over (with Ned Rust)

Middle School, The Worst Years of My Life (with Chris Tebbetts, illustrated by Laura Park)

Daniel X: Demons and Druids (with Adam Sadler)

Daniel X: Watch the Skies (with Ned Rust)

The Dangerous Days of Daniel X (with Michael Ledwidge)

santaKid

MANGA AND GRAPHIC NOVELS

Daniel X: The Manga 1–3 (with SeungHui Kye)

Daniel X: Alien Hunter (with Leopoldo Gout)

Maximum Ride: The Manga 1–8 (with NaRae Lee)

Witch & Wizard: The Manga 1–3 (with Svetlana Chmakova)

Zoo: The Graphic Novel (with Andy MacDonald)

For previews of upcoming books and more information about James Patterson, please visit JamesPatterson.com or find him on Facebook or at your app store.

JAMES PATTERSON
RECOMMENDS

THE #1 BESTSELLER and
THE 1st ALEX CROSS NOVEL

ALONG CAME A SPIDER

JAMES PATTERSON

ALONG CAME A SPIDER

Before the movies and before Alex Cross became a household name, there was ALONG CAME A SPIDER. This is the story that started it all: Alex Cross's game of cat-and-mouse with the deadly serial kidnapper Gary Soneji. He's one of the most terrifying villains I've ever created: the soft-spoken math teacher who makes you feel comfortable enough to entrust your children with him. Until they go missing. If you want to know what the Alex Cross series is all about, there's no better place to start than at the beginning.

JAMES PATTERSON

MARY MARY

MARY, MARY

Alex Cross operates best in the dark, gritty underbelly of society. Which made me want to put him under the bright, shiny lights of Tinseltown. So I did. From Disneyland to places only the rich and famous ever see—that's where I take you in MARY, MARY. This the glossiest, sleekest, most cinematic Alex Cross book to date. Someone is murdering Hollywood's most beautiful A-list actresses. The killer's name? Mary Smith. And, boy, does Mary give a new meaning to being a "diehard" fan.

JAMES
PATTERSON

ALEX CROSS
FACES THE DEADLIEST
PSYCHOPATH
OF THEM ALL—HIS
WIFE'S KILLER

CROSS

ALSO PUBLISHED AS *ALEX CROSS*

CROSS

There was one pressure point in Alex Cross's life that I deliberately left unexplored for the longest time: his wife's unsolved murder. I knew if there was anything that could push him over the edge, it'd be coming face-to-face with his wife's killer. And in CROSS, the timing was right for this most significant encounter. As an ex-FBI agent, Alex knows he should follow the law. As a man whose wife was killed, he can't ignore the sweet call of vengeance. This is the most personal of all of Alex's cases. And the one that could very well make him spiral into a deep, dark place from which he can never return.

Dear Reader:

Aren't you glad you're not Alex Cross? While everyone else gets to gather around the table for a hearty Christmas dinner, he has to chase down bad guys. Fortunately, he's pretty good at his job, so one of Nana Mama's delicious feasts is never too far away.

Nana Mama let me write down some of her best holiday recipes to whip up a tasty and festive spread. By total coincidence, some of these are my favorites, too. Is there such a thing as too much pecan pie?

Enjoy,

HEAVENLY BISCUITS RECIPE

Ingredients:

- 1 package dry yeast
- ¼ cup warm water
- 2½ cups flour, plus additional for kneading
- ½ teaspoon baking soda
- 1 teaspoon baking powder
- 1 teaspoon salt
- 2 tablespoons sugar
- ½ cup shortening
- 1 cup buttermilk

Method:

Dissolve the yeast in the warm water. Set aside. Mix the flour, baking soda, baking powder, salt, and sugar together. Cut in the shortening. Stir in the buttermilk and yeast mixture, and mix thoroughly.

Preheat the oven to 400°F.

Turn the dough out on a floured board and knead

lightly. Roll out the dough about ¾ inch thick and cut with a biscuit cutter. Place the biscuits in a greased pan. Let the dough rise slightly before baking. Bake for 12–15 minutes.

Yield: 12 biscuits

PRALINE SWEET POTATOES

Ingredients:

- 6 medium yams, peeled and boiled until soft, or 2 (40-ounce) cans sweet potatoes, drained and liquid reserved
- ¼ pound (1 stick) butter, melted
- 2 teaspoon salt, divided use
- 1 cup brown sugar, divided use
- 2 teaspoons cinnamon
- 1 teaspoon nutmeg
- ⅓ cup evaporated milk
- ⅓ cup orange juice
- ¼ cup flour
- ⅔ cup firmly packed brown sugar
- 4 tablespoons (½ stick) cold butter
- 1 cup chopped pecans

Method:

Preheat the oven to 350°F.

Mix the yams, melted butter, 1 teaspoon of the salt, ⅓ cup of the brown sugar, cinnamon, nutmeg, evaporated milk, and orange juice until smooth, adding reserved liquid or water if needed for consistency. Pour into a greased casserole dish.

Combine the flour and the remaining ⅔ cup of the brown sugar. Cut in the cold butter until crumbly, then mix in the nuts. Sprinkle the mixture on top of the sweet potatoes. Bake for 30 minutes.

Yield: 8 servings

COLLARD GREENS WITH HAM HOCK

Ingredients:

- 3 quarts water
- ½ pound ham hocks
- 1 tablespoon Nana Mama's Seasoning (recipe below)
- 1 tablespoon seasoned salt
- 2 teaspoons hot red pepper sauce
- 1 large bunch collard greens
- 1 tablespoon butter

Method:

In a large pot, bring the water to a boil. Add the ham hocks, Nana Mama's Seasoning, seasoned salt, and hot sauce. Reduce the heat to medium and let simmer for 1 hour.

Wash the collard greens thoroughly. Remove the stems that run down the center by holding the leaf in your left hand and stripping the leaf down with your right hand. There is no need to strip the tender leaves in the heart of the collards. Stack 6–8 leaves on top of one another, roll up, and slice into ½- to 1-inch-thick slices. Add the greens and butter to the pot, and simmer for additional 45–60 minutes, stirring occasionally.

Yield: 4–6 servings

NANA MAMA'S SEASONING

Ingredients:

- 1 cup salt
- ¼ cup black pepper
- ¼ cup garlic powder
- 2 tablespoons paprika

Method:

Mix all ingredients together and store in an airtight container for up to 6 months.

OLD FASHIONED GLAZED HAM

Ingredients:

- ¾ cup Dijon mustard
- ¾ cup light brown sugar, plus more for sprinkling
- 1 tablespoon chopped fresh thyme leaves
- 1 (14-pound) cooked and smoked cured ham, shank end
- ¾ cup pineapple juice
- 20 canned pineapple rings
- 20 maraschino cherries

Method:

Preheat the oven to 350°F. Put the oven rack in the middle of the oven.

In a small bowl, mix together the Dijon mustard, brown sugar, and thyme.

Put the ham in a large roasting pan, fat side up. Rub the ham with the mustard glaze, and pour the pineapple juice into the bottom of the pan. Bake for 2 hours, brushing every 20 minutes with the pineapple juice. Remove the ham from the oven and increase the heat to 400°F.

Using toothpicks, add the pineapple rings to the ham, putting a cherry in the center of each pineapple ring. Lightly sprinkle the pineapple rings with brown sugar. Return the ham to the oven and bake until the pineapples turn a light golden brown. Transfer the ham to a serving platter and let rest for 15 minutes before serving.

Yield: 10–12 servings

PECAN PIE

Ingredients:

Crust

- 4 tablespoons (½ stick) unsalted butter, cubed
- 4 ounces pecan halves or pieces
- ¾ cup all-purpose flour, plus additional for rolling
- ½ teaspoon kosher salt
- 2 tablespoons ice water
- 2 tablespoons bourbon, chilled

Filling

- 3 large eggs
- ½ cup sugar
- ½ cup golden syrup
- 4 tablespoons (½ stick) unsalted butter, melted and cooled slightly
- 1 tablespoon bourbon
- 1 teaspoon vanilla extract
- ¼ teaspoon kosher salt
- 8 ounces Spiced Pecans, divided use (recipe below)

Method:

To make the crust:
Chill the butter in the freezer for 15 minutes.

Pulse the pecans 6–7 times in a food processor or until finely ground. Add the flour and salt, and pulse an additional 4–5 times. Add the butter and pulse several more times until the mixture looks mealy. Add the water and bourbon, and pulse 5–6 times until the mixture holds together when squeezed and feels like dough. Transfer the dough to a gallon-sized zip-top bag, squeeze together until it forms a ball, then press into a disk and refrigerate for 30 minutes.

To assemble and bake the pie:
Heat the oven to 350°F.

Whisk the eggs, sugar, golden syrup, butter, bourbon, vanilla, and salt together until combined. Set aside.

Remove the dough from the refrigerator and let it sit at room temperature for 5 minutes. Remove the dough from the bag and sprinkle both sides very lightly with flour. Use a rolling pin to form an 11-inch circle. Sprinkle the top of the dough with more flour and place it into a pan. Gently press the dough into the sides of the pan, crimping and trimming the edges as necessary.

Coarsely chop 6 ounces of the Spiced Pecans and evenly sprinkle them in the crust. Pour the filling on top. Bake for 20 minutes. Arrange the remaining 2 ounces of whole pecans in a border on the edge of the filling. Bake 10 more minutes, until a skewer inserted in the center comes out clean (the center of the pie should reach 200°F). Cool on a cooling rack to room temperature before serving, 3½–4 hours.

Yield: 1 pie, 8 servings

SPICED PECANS

Ingredients:

- 1 teaspoon kosher salt
- ½ teaspoon ground cumin
- ¼ teaspoon cayenne pepper
- ½ teaspoon ground cinnamon
- ½ teaspoon dried ground orange peel
- 1 pound pecan halves
- 4 tablespoons (½ stick) unsalted butter
- ¼ cup packed light brown sugar
- 2 tablespoons packed dark brown sugar
- 2 tablespoons water

Method:

Line a half sheet pan with parchment paper and set aside.

Mix the salt, cumin, cayenne, cinnamon, and orange peel together in a bowl and set aside.

In a pan over medium-high heat, stir the nuts for 4–5 minutes until they just start to brown and smell toasted. Add the butter and stir until it melts. Add the spice mixture and stir to combine. Once combined, add the sugars and water, stirring until the mixture thickens and coats the nuts, about 2 minutes.

Transfer the nuts to the prepared sheet pan and separate them with a fork or spatula. Allow the nuts to cool completely before transferring to an airtight container for storage. Can be stored for up to 3 weeks.